I0572480

The Oz Suite

Gerard Houarner

'The Oz Suite'
Gerard Houarner

Copyright 2008. No part of this publication may be reproduced by any means, electronic or mechanical, without prior permission from the author.

Published in 2008 by Eibonvale Press
www.eibonvalepress.co.uk

Cover art and interior/exterior design by David Rix
www.eibonvale.co.uk

Printed by Lightning Source
www.lightningsource.com

No We Love No One previously appeared in the anthology 'Dammed: An Anthology of the Lost', Necro Publications 2004

ISBN
978-0-9555268-3-1

To the flying monkeys in all of us

Acknowledgements to Dave Barnett
and to David Rix, for taking leaps of
faith in my use and abuse of Oz

Contents

No
We
Love
No
One

They came down from the sky one night like baby spiders cast to the winds, tucked into pearlescent spiral shells suspended from parachutes made of no earthly silk.

The children. Newborns, back then. In all the colors of human flesh.

Their mysterious mothers, or mother, did not announce or claim them as they floated down on to cities and towns; lonely houses and camp sites and caves; and even cars and jets and tanks and beasts of burden. I found out later the shells found submarine and missile silo crews in their depths of sea and earth, religious hermits who had lost themselves in deserts and mountains, the insane in their asylums, the criminals in jails, everyone, wherever they sheltered for that day's turning from the sun. The shells stuck to doors and windows and hatches and rocks, on and beneath the ground and the sea, in the air, miraculously adapting to their environment so that no harm would come to their contents or to their nearby adoptive parent.

I remember that's how it began. As simple as that. No explanation, at least, none that Dad and his new wife Doris could understand. Dad was like that big guy in war movies who carries the heaviest gun but needs the smart little guy to tell him where to shoot. He'd shake his head and frown the same way for a flat tire and a death in the family, like every troubling event, no matter how great or small, reflected the same great mystery. My Mom wanted more out of life than an unwanted child and someone else's profound sense of awe for life's challenges, and left us both. The woman he found afterwards didn't mind his consistent approach to existence. But she didn't have any answers, either.

Like the universe, the shells simply appeared one day, delivering their burdens to every living man and woman. Me and Silas got off, of course, along with everyone else under sixteen: even whoever made all those babies didn't trust us kids.

I was the first in the house to see them come down. Silas was asleep. Doris was online talking to her sister and Dad was in the living room reading a science magazine. I was looking out the window, bored with games, TV, books, homework, everything. I liked looking into the dark places between the street lights, under the trees between houses at night, because my mind could fill the darkness with so much more than what I could see was real in the light.

Something passed under the street lamps a few houses up the street, making a moving shadow on the road. I thought it was a bat. Something knocked against the siding on the other side of the house. Doris called for him to go look. She knew better than to wonder out loud about the noise and set off a few minutes of frozen pondering. Across the street, a circular, shining shape I thought at first was a new kind of cable dish collided with the house near the top of its pitched roof, slid down and came to rest outside the upstairs bedroom window. The chute hung limp all the way to the ground.

I took out my binoculars and studied the dish. It looked like a snail shell, only as big as a computer monitor, shimmering white with just a hint of colors I couldn't put a name to. Pearlescent was a word I picked out of the news reports, later.

"I thought it was a lie," Silas said, suddenly next to me.

I jumped a little, but I didn't think he noticed. He hadn't scared me deliberately. He wasn't like that. *His* mom made sure he was nothing like me. "What," I said, looking at other houses up and down the street. There were shells on a few, and I could make out the parachutes floating out of the sky like pale tree blossoms, going down the street right above the lamps and maneuvering to the left and right like they were homing in on particular addresses.

"The stork. Dropping babies from the sky."

"Yeah. That's a lie." I put the binoculars down. Something else bumped into the house. Doris called for Dad again, but I could hear him coming up the stairs.

"So what's this?"

Silas smelled sweaty and felt hot standing next to me, like the funk and heat from running around all day had suddenly caught up to him. "I don't know," I said with a deliberate little catch in my voice, turning away.

He looked at me. Started crying. I offered him the binoculars but that's not what he wanted. He tried to take my free hand, but I held the binoculars with both hands, in front of me so he couldn't grab a comforting hug.

A part of me felt good. I liked scaring Silas. His fright made me feel like I'd done something important with my life, like I'd taught him a little piece of the truth. Some day all those pieces would come together in his head, and he'd stop running back to his Mom and our Dad like it was safer with them. Some day he'd know what I already knew at 12, that they were worse than me or anything else he'd run into out in the world. And they didn't even mean to be.

You're never more alive than when you're scared. Not having sex or eating warm cookies and cold milk. Fear is death, and death so close it's living inside makes you realize you're alive.

That's what I wanted to give Silas, even though he didn't deserve it. He was still my half-brother.

Dad was the one who found David. That's what he named the baby boy he took out of the shell stuck to the side of the house that night outside the master bedroom window. He stared at the pale, wet human shape kicking and wiggling in his hands, peered into the boy's wide open eyes, and said, "Hello, David," like he'd met a long lost buddy. "Meet your new baby brother, boys," he said, giving us a wink.

It didn't bother him too much that the next thing David did was start eating the string between the shell and the chute. Dad tried to stop him, even asked Silas and me to pick up that stuff off the bedroom floor and take it outside. Neither of us moved closer than the bedroom doorway. Doris came up from behind, but didn't go in either. Instead, she grabbed Silas' shoulders like she was ready to snatch him out of a train wreck.

"There's another one on the other side of the window," Dad said, giving her a glance, then putting all of his attention on the infant in his arms. He tried putting his fingers over David's mouth, then gently pushed back the baby's entangled hands, but the boy cried and squirmed like Dad was ripping out an intestine. He finally let the baby have his way, setting him on the floor. Dad shook his head, his face contorting into the usual pained expression when the boy went back to eating, this time grabbing hold of the shell that had delivered him. Another attempt at stopping and distracting the boy made him scream so loud all of us, even Dad, took a step back and let him have his way.

David came with a mouthful of teeth, the strength to crack and chew shell that wouldn't break any other way, and the determination to finish eating everything that had brought him to us.

Other screams came from neighboring houses. Some sounded like babies. Others, from adults.

While the boy ate, Dad brought in the other shell and gave it to Doris. She didn't want to take it, but a baby head poked out of the opening and fixed a pair of blue eyes on her. Doris took the shell, though her whole body shook. Silas tried to hang on to her and started up crying again. She pushed Silas away, then shoved him to me. Before Silas could throw himself at her again, she went upstairs to the attic and locked the door behind her.

None of us ever saw that baby, its shell or its chute, ever again.

With nothing else to do, we watched David eat. Dad, because he cared. Silas, because he was scared and me and Dad were there. Me, I wanted to keep an eye on what was going on. When David was done, Dad picked him up and took him downstairs, telling us to follow. We all sat around the television in the living room and watched the news. Silas cuddled with me, wouldn't let go of my arm. I let him have his way, figuring he was getting better lessons than I could ever give him just from what was happening. Dad held David in his arms, rocking him occasionally, putting a towel between him and the baby's bottom just in case something leaked out. He mentioned something about going to the store for pampers, but between the baby and the TV, he stayed pinned to the couch.

That baby never leaked. Didn't cry, either. Just stared with eyes as big as shark mouths at Dad.

About an hour into the special news reports preempting all programming, Doris came downstairs, avoiding the living room on her way to the kitchen and then the yard. By then, the neighborhood was up in arms. Dad was busy on the phone and not paying attention to Doris, or to Silas and me.

She spent forty-five minutes out there, in the dark. It sounded like she was digging. Neither of us left the house to see what was going on.

Police cruisers, with sirens on and lights flashing, passed by along with cars and trucks. People ran back and forth, shouting, yelling, cursing, weeping. On television, men and women dressed like school principals talked a lot. A live shot came up showing the shells attaching themselves to the sides of buildings, next to windows; then another, showing the shells around the hatch of an airliner that had made an emergency landing.

Doris came back alone. She took Silas by the hand. He didn't want to let go of me, and I fought a little to keep him, just to make things interesting. "Don't let her do the same thing to you," I whispered into his ear before letting go. Doris took him up to bed without a word, ignoring me and Dad.

I watched the news, waiting to see if anyone would send me to bed. Nobody did. I picked up a few things from the news bulletins. Scientists came on to say the materials found with the babies weren't from our world, or even our universe. The babies appeared physically human, though far more mature than normal infants. And there was always the exact number of babies in their shells for the adults in a house, or a ship or submarine, or a tent, or whatever the shells landed on. Reporters came on from all around the world, confirming previous rumors from the Middle East that the rain of babies had started there and swept across Europe in the middle of the night. Most of the reporters carried their own babies in their arms, staring into the camera with stunned desperation, as if pleading for contributions to a children's charity.

There was talk of invasion, body snatchers, mutants, plagues, clones, miracles, divine retribution, though the babies had done nothing harmful or dangerous. None of them could talk, and no messages had been found in the spiral pattern on the shells or woven into the chutes.

From Dad's conversations, I picked up that things more terrible than babies falling out of the sky were also happening. He argued with relatives about what they had done or were planing to do with their foundlings. Smoke, like from a barbecue, drifted through the street. A big bonfire had been lit up a block over, and the flames sometimes jumped higher than the roofs of the surrounding houses.

The screaming had stopped. The streets were empty. And quiet.

Military men replaced the scientists, ministers, philosophers and other speakers on the newscasts. Reporters stopped appearing on camera with infants. By the time I finally went up to bed on my own, new rules had been laid down: everyone had to turn over the babies to the authorities. Special centers were being set up. Warnings were issued about harmful biological interactions between newcomers and humans. And even if they were safe, the babies were members of the largest illegal mass migration the world had ever known. The source and purpose of this migration had to be discovered. Forms needed to be filed, screenings performed, licences granted.

I went to sleep knowing the world considered these babies dangerous. I loved the little ones for that. Nobody understood how, but everyone agreed they posed a threat. I wasn't so sure about Dad talking like David was going to stay with us. I wasn't at all sure about living with a menace all the time.

When Mom, my Mom, left, I thought it was because she didn't want me. When Dad and Doris came together, I thought Dad wanted her more than me, and when they had Silas, I thought he was what they wanted. But I guess Silas wasn't quite right, either, at least not compared to David. At least, for Dad.

I'm not sure how Dad convinced Doris to keep David. Her baby had still been alive when she buried it, though later she said it wasn't. I know I heard it crying through the earth the next day. I didn't dig it up.

She told us she took the baby upstairs to have a

look at it, tried to breast feed it, but it died, choking on that damned shell, and she was sorry and scared and she buried the body in the backyard along with the shell and the chute. The baby was always an it, never a boy or a girl, which I figured was worse than what I was.

Doris wasn't the only one. Lots of people buried them, or put them in trash disposals or even wood chippers. Whole neighborhoods started up bonfires. Used them for target practice. The babies were cute, very nearly human, but something about watching them eat that shell basket and silk turned on a different instinct in people.

Lots of people kept them, too. The kids were smart, they made it easy. David was talking after a few days. I could hear him and Dad upstairs. He'd make all kinds of soft, wet noises, too, and stuff that almost sounded like laughing, and he never cried or made a fuss. Since he already had teeth, it was easy feeding him. Nothing made him sick. I know, I tried. Just to see. I don't think I could've killed him that way even if I'd tried. And he fought like crazy when his face was covered by a pillow. When people did away with theirs, they had to work.

Doris argued with Dad a lot about keeping David during the first week after David arrived, always bringing up the trouble we could get into keeping him. But he wore her down with his unconditional acceptance, and she said she'd take care of Dad's little shell boy the same she took care of hers.

Then she said she was leaving.

But she didn't do that either. Maybe Doris didn't have anyplace to go, or maybe she felt she and

Silas were safer with Dad than alone or with anyone else. Especially the way things were going in the world. Maybe she stayed to see if Dad was right, if David would someday become all the way human.

People keeping those babies stuck together. I knew the circle in the neighborhood from who Dad talked to every day. Pretty soon, no one worried about what color or religion was trying to move in or out of town, or how high the taxes were going, or how many teachers had been hired in the school district this year. All anybody talked about was who had a baby. And how.

The news talked about conspiracy, and investigations were started to find out who was helping people slip by with their phoney kids. But half the investigators were sympathetic or had babies of their own. Politicians warned about the danger of babies splitting up families, communities, the whole country. Revolutions and crackdowns were starting up on every continent. Countries were ready to go to war over the treatment of kids from the sky.

In our house, war never broke out after that first week. Doris and Dad didn't talk about David much. They hardly talked, period. Dad did everything for David. Sometimes, we wouldn't see them for days. Dad went to work early in the morning, came home late, with David. When he was home, he'd keep David out of the way in the master bedroom. Doris didn't bring him out to play with us after she moved to the attic.

We celebrated the holidays, and birthdays for me and Silas, but not with any kind of happiness. I didn't pay much attention to David, but it was a relief when him and Dad went out and did whatever it was they did together.

I missed Dad at first. But I'd already gone through all of that with Mom. And it wasn't like he was really gone, like Mom. I saw him around, and he still asked me how things were going, and even invited me to come along with him and David. I said no, and he didn't push. David hardly looked at me, and never spoke to anyone but Dad.

Doris might've felt sorry for me. She paid a lot more attention to the way I dressed, and did my homework, and how much time I spent watching television and listening to music. She was especially concerned about who I hung out with at school, and what kinds of questions people asked me, and how me and Silas were treated by teachers and kids.

With Dad hardly there and Doris always around, I had to be careful with Silas. Instead of stealing or breaking things he liked, or watching him without talking until he freaked, or telling him lies about Doris and Dad and family and neighbors, I cut out pictures from magazines or downloaded and printed them from sites about the shell kids and what was happening to them. I left the pictures for him to find in his bed, school books, comics, wherever. Sometimes Doris would find one and scream at him, really loud, while she was crying.

Silas never said anything about me planting them. He was too scared of what was in the pictures, and of his Mom.

Folks stopped talking about the new children on television and programs got back to normal. Eventually, it got harder to find pictures of what adults had done to the children that night, and what they were doing to them in other countries. But I worked hard at the job. I liked what I saw in Silas.

After things settled down, Dad left later for work, came home earlier, spent more time around the house on weekends. Kids stopped asking about my new baby brother, trying to beat me up for it, or reporting me to the teachers and counselors and principal because I was harboring a fugitive, the way they liked to say it. Dad and David started eating dinner with us most evenings. We went out once together as a family to a movie. I noticed there were a lot of kids David's age in the crowd for that showing, like everyone who'd kept their extra had made an appointment to be there at that time, in a display of togetherness. You couldn't tell the real kids from the shell ones, who were walking around like they were 3 or 4 already. Then the movie started. Silas and me and the ones like us couldn't sit still. It was a grown-up movie, with talking and kissing, and who cared about that? But David and his kind sat there and took it all in without a sound. It wasn't natural. Doris looked scared when the lights came up. But Dad, he was as proud as anything and gave David a hug. He wasn't the only one.

One day, about a year after the night the babies came down from the sky, I came home and found Silas outside in the yard.

"He's in there," Silas said, looking at the trees and the sky and the clouds, like he was searching for something else to fall out of the sky.

"If you're out here, does that mean he took your

place?" I asked, and almost laughed at the look Silas gave me.

I found David inside, alone, watching TV. Without Dad next to him, it hit me how big he'd gotten, half as big as Silas.

David looked away from the screen, gave me a smile, and said, "Hi." Then he went back to watching. Silly, old-fashioned music filled the house like plastic flowers, and what he was looking at hit me: *The Wizard of Oz*. We had it on disk, though I hadn't seen it in years. I was way too old for that stuff by then.

David, though, was lost in the movie. He sat there with his mouth hanging open a little, like a kid who's gotten just enough of his favorite ice cream, and everything he ever wanted on Christmas and his birthday, and had every day of the year to play without ever having to worry about tests and homework and high school kids waiting to beat you up, much less a Mom and Dad leaving you.

I sat down and watched him instead of the movie. He didn't mind. The movie's colors flowed over his face, giving it more life than I'd ever seen in any of those children. His eyes flicked all over the place, like he was following different things in the background, things we didn't usually notice because we were looking at the main characters or the action. I tried to see if he looked like Dad, or Doris, or Mom. Then I tried to match him up to kids I knew at school, and ones I'd seen on TV. But he didn't look like anyone I'd ever known. I couldn't smell him, either, or feel his presence on the couch, in the room. It was like he was invisible, a ghost, without substance.

"You like that movie?" I asked, studying his face.

"Yes," he answered, softly. "It's so beautiful and wonderful." His eyes were shiny, like he was about to cry. I'd never seen him give up tears.

I remembered kids his true age shouldn't be able to talk like he was doing. "Who do you like best?"

He frowned a little, like he was thinking hard.

"I bet it's Dorothy, right?" I said. "Because she fell into Oz like you fell into here, out of nowhere. She didn't belong in Oz, like you don't here. And she's a sissy girl who thought she was special because a good witch gave her magic shoes. But where are your magic shoes, David? And how are you going to go back home if there's no Yellow Brick road to follow?"

I got up, stopped the disk player, took out the movie, smashed it to pieces under my heel. Then I gave him what was left and asked, "Do you know who the bad witch is?"

He just stared at me, without a smile or a frown. His eyes stayed dry. There wasn't a trace of fear in him.

I forgot all about Silas after that. David infected me like a virus. I couldn't stop thinking about him, what he was under that skin, what thoughts were going through that brain. What he felt, if anything. I knew Silas was human. I'd seen enough of his fear. But what was David? I guess it's the same question that made people like my Dad take his kind in, or drove others like Doris to kill them. I had a feeling David didn't know who or what he was, or what he was doing here, or what being alive meant. I'd never seen him want anything, or be afraid, or even really laugh. I wanted to help him find out who he was, so we would both know. He needed my help.

I took my time. Dad bought replacement copies of the Wizard of Oz, and I made sure something always happened to them. I snuck into Dad's bedroom, when David was in there alone, and asked questions: What did his real mommy and daddy look like? Why did they dump him with us? What did he do that was so bad he had to be sent so far away? Was he ever going back? Did anyone love him? Really love him, like a mom and dad? Did he know what happened to all his brothers and sisters? The ones he didn't see when he went out with Dad? What was going to happen to him when he got older? Was he going to be stuck here forever, without a job, all alone, no family or friends? Or was he going to disappear one day, vanish like he appeared? Would anybody miss him?

He never answered any questions. He never showed any pain or fear or amusement. It was like I was talking to the steel front doors at school when they were locked shut.

I showed him every version of *Invasion of the Body Snatchers* and *Village of the Damned* I could find, and movies like them. He watched, but only *The Wizard of Oz* had any effect on him.

There were times when I caught him staring at nothing. I'd stand in his line of sight, and I felt a chill, and then I broke into a sweat, but I wouldn't move. One night, when Dad was away on a business trip, we stayed like that until morning, when Doris found me and dragged me away to go to school.

I collected more pictures and stories about what was happening to the other children all over the world: how they were still being hunted down and killed for sport, or sold into slavery for labor or sex, or how some rich people collected them, like fossils or baseball cards or paintings. There were rumors about military and corporate and underground research facilities with their studies and experiments, and religious fanatics setting kids up as saints and gods, or sacrificing them as devils. I made sure David saw them all.

Then I told him the scientists were coming. Or the slavers. Or the collectors. I'd call the house constantly when I knew he was alone, or cut school and ring the doorbell and hide.

Still, I got no reaction out of him.

It took another year for David to pass Silas in size, and come up on me in age by the way he acted. By then, all the shell kids were coming out from hiding. Though there were differences in height and weight, under the different skin colors and hair styles and sexes they had a sameness. It was almost a walk, or the way they turned their heads, or a faint accent. But not quite. It was like a sound humans couldn't hear but knew was there, a sound only animals heard. That year, *The Wizard of Oz* was a world wide best seller. "Somewhere Over the Rainbow" was the number one song on the pop charts.

The children never hung out with each other. Only a few were with kids like me, who were given the responsibility of their care while walking around. Mostly, they stayed by themselves, walking around parks and malls. Cops sometimes picked them up.

Gangs of kids chased them, but you never saw anything really bad happen.

Since I always had to be with David, I tried to set up a kidnaping. But with so many roaming around, anybody who wanted a shell kid could find one without going through so much trouble. I got some older high school kids to attack us. We both got beat up pretty bad, a few times, David more than me. But like in the other incidents I saw, no one had the nerve or heart to kill David, or at least try hard at doing him, like I wanted. Dad just locked us both up for a few months afterwards. Some adults gave us a hard time, not letting us into stores or yelling at us in the street, but nothing came of it.

David took the beatings the same way he took being kept in the house, or insulted by adults, or refused service in a restaurant, or not allowed to use the bathroom. He didn't smile and he didn't cry, just walked away.

Dad wanted to register David in school, but the administrators wouldn't take him, and the lawyers who came to fight the case couldn't force the issue. David didn't have rights.

I hardly ever talked to Silas, anymore. David being taller than him was more than enough to keep him on edge. His education was no longer my priority. But one night, Doris stopped by my bed after she'd said good night to Silas. She put a hand on my shoulder, and whispered in my ear like I used to do to her son:

"What do they see when they stare off into nothing? What do they see when they look in the mirror? What do they see when they look at us?"

Her breath was so hot it scorched my ear, and every word came out like a knife dipped in venom. She didn't wait for an answer. As she left, I saw her face in the night light and it was hard, and the last look she gave me before she went through the door put ice in my veins.

Silas had told his mother everything I used to do to him. Maybe he was trying to tell her I was handling the situation, or he missed my attention, or maybe he'd figured out how much fun I had torturing him by watching me with David and he wanted some measure of revenge. Maybe he'd seen that I had no effect on David, and I no longer intimidated him. He'd certainly become more scared of David than of me. I shouldn't have forgotten about him, I should have reminded him of what I could so, what it felt like for a human to be under my attention.

It was the first time I'd felt so afraid I couldn't sleep. I was more alive than I had ever been.

Not long after that episode, David spun his first shell. Dad brought it down from the bedroom and showed it to us while we were eating dinner. He held it up proudly, like he once did with a diorama I did in second grade, or with Silas' first piece of writing.

Doris screamed. Silas ran out and didn't come home for a day. I went upstairs while Dad and Doris went out to look for him.

"What are you doing?" I asked David, who was sitting cross-legged at the foot of the bed, moving his hands around a pale white lump of something like clay in his lap.

David didn't answer. But he smiled. And his

hands moved round and round, and I could see every now and then, when the angle was right, moist white threads shooting out from under his fingernails, and while I was trying to get a better look at that I didn't pay attention to what he was actually making until it was almost finished: a shell, the size of a soccer ball, smaller but still spiral and catching colors on the inside lip, like the one that brought him to us.

"Are you going to eat it, now?" I asked. "Or are you getting ready to make some babies?" I picked up one of the shells he'd already finished and put it to my mouth. I was ready to take a bite, but the smell of it – like a tidal pool at the beach filled with sea weed – made me gag. I threw it down, breaking off a small chip.

David looked up at me. The smile was gone.

That night, Doris left. I didn't hear her go out, though I'd heard her and Dad come back from the police station to report Silas being gone. She didn't even wait for her boy to come back. Silas came home early in the morning and woke me up to ask where his Mom was, and we went up to the attic. She wasn't there but all her clothes and stuff and even money was laying around. Dad came up to look. Then he went back to the police station with Silas. I stayed home from school, alone in the house with David.

"Did you see her go?" I asked him. When he didn't look up from making another shell, I asked, "Did you make her go?" When he still didn't answer, I asked, "Did you do something to her?" That's when he looked to me for a moment. My heart skipped because I thought I'd finally broken through and hit a vulnerable point, a place he and his kind shared with the rest of us.

But his expression didn't change. It was like he'd heard a fly buzz in and out of the room. He went back to his work like I wasn't there. I noticed he'd gotten bigger. A lot bigger. He was past high school size, getting thick like boys sometimes did in college.

The news was crazy with mass disappearances. More people than just Doris had vanished in the middle of the night. The President was gone. So were a lot of important scientists, businessmen, artists. War broke out between more than a few countries. A few small nukes went off, and some biological weapons were used. More people died. In between those big stories were the little ones about hunting parties – official and unofficial -- going after the shell kids, and massacres of children taking place. Almost all of those killed were not shell kids, reports were saying.

I wasn't scared. Things were going as I'd always thought they might. Even being alone in the house with David didn't bother me. I remembered a nature show, about reef sharks swimming around during the day, being harassed by other fish. Come night, those sharks turned and became killers, devouring everything in the water. If David was a shark, I didn't think night had come, at least for me. And if it did, I was sure I could find cover, like the smart reef fish did.

Dad and Silas came home. Silas wouldn't stop crying. Dad left him with me while he went to stock up on food and water. "I told you," I said to Silas. I thought for sure Silas was next to go. I think he did, too. I didn't have to say more to keep him raw and in pain.

But it wasn't him that was next, it was Dad. A few nights later. David's last night in the house. I woke up to go to the bathroom, and something told me to look in on Dad. David was in there, by himself, making shells. The room was three-quarter filled with them. I looked all over the house, in the basement, outside, but I couldn't find Dad. There wasn't a note or a message on the phone. The car was in the garage, his shoes by the door.

I didn't miss Dad as much as I thought I would. A lot of him had been gone for a while, already, so his body not being in the house didn't bother me too much. Silas went hysterical. He came out after I'd done my search. He must have seen something in my face and went straight to the bedroom, understanding before I did what had happened. What David had done.

He ran through house screaming and crying in every room like it was religious duty. I knocked him out with a bat to the head and left him bleeding in the living room while I went back upstairs. I didn't quite know what I was going to do when I went into the bedroom, but after smashing most of the shells I stopped and stared at David. He was full grown, standing by a dresser full of Dad's clothes, which he was wearing, too. I think he could've taken the bat away from me with no problem. He sure wasn't scared of me.

"What did you do to them?" I asked. I glanced at a portrait of Dad and Doris on a dresser table, looked again, to see if they hadn't been magically captured behind the glass, like on a TV horror show.

David didn't answer, he just walked out like I wasn't there. Like I didn't matter, could never reach inside to touch the thing he had in common with me and everyone else born to this world. He was gone by the time I got downstairs.

Things went completely crazy everywhere. People shot each other over babies and kids, or killed any baby or kid they thought came from someplace else. It didn't matter that most of the shell kids looked like adults by now. They still weren't real, but they could pass much easier.

I took care of things for a while. Made ends meet. Silas stayed around for a month. The cut I gave him never healed properly, settling into a nasty scar. He never spoke to me, but did do what I told him to. He was scared all the time, and I didn't even have to do anything to him. There were plenty of guns around the house, for protection, and I'd used them and shown Silas how to shoot, just in case. But he never dared pull one on me, even just to try to shake me up. Then he was gone, too. I don't know if he ran away, or if David came back and got him. I didn't care.

Emergency services eventually took over, and order was restored. I got through what I had to get through to keep the house and get as much of Dad's money as I could and collect insurance and benefits and such. Things quieted down. There were long lines for everything everywhere. I got a draft number, but wasn't old enough for the new compulsory military service, yet. I had to have a physical, though, and an ID card to prove I wasn't one of those other children, like everyone else. Things started running again, though nothing like how they were before.

Television wasn't on much. Newspapers and

magazines didn't come out so often. The internet was tough to reach no matter which way you tried connecting. Radio became the big thing, but the news the stations carried didn't say much about what was really going on.

Now, if this was just a story I was telling, I'd say the end came when started I making shells from jets of clay coming out from under my fingernails, and the kids who came down that night went popping off into another universe through a hole I didn't know I could make until bunches of them started showing up at my doorstep. Or maybe I went somewhere, to the center of the earth, or the tallest mountain, or an island, and met the momma spider, or spiders, that made all those the children, and I was adopted, or maybe caught in momma's web, and the spiders are about to kill me and I'm telling you this as the last words I'll ever speak. Or there's always the one where I can feel David coming for me, like a shark, and I'm caught at night in the open on the reef, and there's no place to hide, and I can see his mouth open wide, wider, wi----

But none of that is true.

David did find me, but it was broad daylight on a clear summer's day and I never felt or even saw him coming. He walked up to me while I was working street maintenance downtown for my government check, on a block by myself. He had no reason to know I'd be there. It was like a shark tracking down prey from miles away on the faintest trace of blood on a current.

"Are you staying a while?" I asked, leaning against the shovel, thinking I could throw gravel in his face and then come around and smack him with the blade if he made a move. I was also thinking I could keep him from saying anything I didn't want to hear by speaking first.

"You know, we're not staying much longer," he said.

"Oh." I had to look up at him, like he really was my father and I was a little kid again, and he was telling me Mom had left.

Voices rose in a familiar, rhythmic chant a block away, out of sight around a corner. The chant, and the sound of marching, echoed in the modest downtown canyons where hardly any vehicles passed anymore. A chill passed through me, though I was hot and sweaty from working on the road.

"It's getting time to move on."

A scientist or reporter would've asked where to, and how. And why they needed to stop off here in the first place. Me, I just said, "Not a minute too soon," then wiped sweat from my face.

"We'll miss this place. I'll miss you."

"What?" That last part shook me up. Nobody ever told me they'd miss me. People just left.

"You gave me what I needed," David said.

"What was that?" I didn't really want to hear the answer. What I wanted was to get rid of the sick feeling I had in my gut, the heaviness on my shoulders and in my legs, the ache twisting in my chest.

The sound of marching came closer. Shadows bobbed against the sunlit facade of a building on the opposite corner of the nearest cross-street. The stamping feet accompanying the rising chant drove it deeper into my head, until suddenly I remembered where it came from: the Wizard of Oz. The stupid, wordless song accompanying the Wicked Witch of the West's guards as they trooped into her castle. I shook my head, wondering if somebody was playing a joke on me, but then I got dizzy and it took everything I had not to go down on one knee and close my eyes.

David didn't try to help me, but he did answer my question. "Your kind gave us the certainty that, though we were ruin to who and what we met, we could be innocent, as well."

"Are you angels?" I asked, reaching into my pocket to relieve some of the weight pulling me down. I took out the pistol I carried to protect myself, even though the supervisors told us we weren't supposed to have them because the military controlled the streets. I didn't think those were soldiers marching around the corner.

"Not angels, or devils," David said, looking past me to the source of the sounds coming closer. "We were not more than what you are, and became what you might yet be, if you're ever cast out and made into the mirror for another kind."

I pointed the gun at him and took a shot, then five more, each blast dimmer, as if I was losing hearing, or the powder in the bullets had lost its potency. The bullets hit David in a tight pattern on his chest. At least a couple of them had to have passed through his heart. I put my hand down, feeling the barrel's heat against my skin through my pants leg. Pulling the trigger the first time had lightened the burden I felt I was carrying, but when David didn't go down and I kept shooting, the weight piled on top of me until I couldn't do anything, not even fall down. I was locked into place, a statue, a memorial to what I'd always been.

The marchers rounded the corner, men and women just like David, swinging their arms easily, lifting their knees a little with every step, marching in perfect rhythm, left, right, left, like they were happy to be together and going where they wanted to and serving the cause that had brought them all together. And as they came nearer, there was movement in the windows, in the garbage dumpsters, in the tree branches and garden plots around fountains and building entries, behind sewer gratings and dust piles gathered at the back of dead-end alleys. Figures appeared out of these same places I'd seen on television and the internet, where the shell children had been lynched from trees and light posts, or tossed from windows, or burned to ashes in great fires, or murdered by mobs and thrown out with the rest of the day's refuse, or buried. I imagined the small plot in the backyard of our house, where Doris had buried her infant, and I saw the earth stirring, parting, little hands clawing through to the surface, a tiny body pulling itself out of a hole.

I looked for the infants scurrying to keep up with the older children, though they should not have been able to walk at their apparent age.

I searched for the child my own mother might have gotten rid of, knowing she already had a son she'd left behind so there was no reason to keep a new one.

But, of course, I found no other half-brothers or sisters.

The column passed. The massed voice of their chanting shook me. I realized the chant was more than musical sounds: it had words, and the phrase the formed had a meaning. I wondered how they could have picked out the phrase from the movie. David moved to join his brothers and sisters, the holes in his chest like windows, not bleeding, not letting the life drain out of him, just allowing light and air through their emptiness.

"Take me with you," I said, wanting to take his hand, needing him to pull me along with him.

"I can't," David said, shouting, his feet already in rhythm with the column at his back. "You were our redemption. You have to find your own." And then he was gone, merged into the mass, another figure passing through my life, leaving me behind with nothing but words couched in the sing song tune from an old movie ringing in the air:

NO WE LOVE NO ONE, NO WE LOVE NO ONE, NO WE LOVE NO ONE

And I was never more frightened, and never felt more alive, than when I was left behind with whatever my sins might be, and theirs.

But the question that bleeds me like a wound that will never heal, that makes me tell this story over and over like Sisyphus pushing his damned rock, is did children who fell from the sky sing those words for themselves, or for those of us they left behind?

I'm tired of being alive, and scared. Death lives inside me, but it has also left me behind. I chant the shell children's words as they did, but no one, not even death, comes back to claim me. There are no spider mothers to embrace me, no witches wicked or good, no Yellow Brick Road or a wizard with secrets.

I wonder when my penance will be done, and

my turn will come to be the mirror for another kind, so I can find my innocence and my redemption. I wonder if you, if anyone or anything, will ever hear me, no matter how many chants I sing or stories I tell.

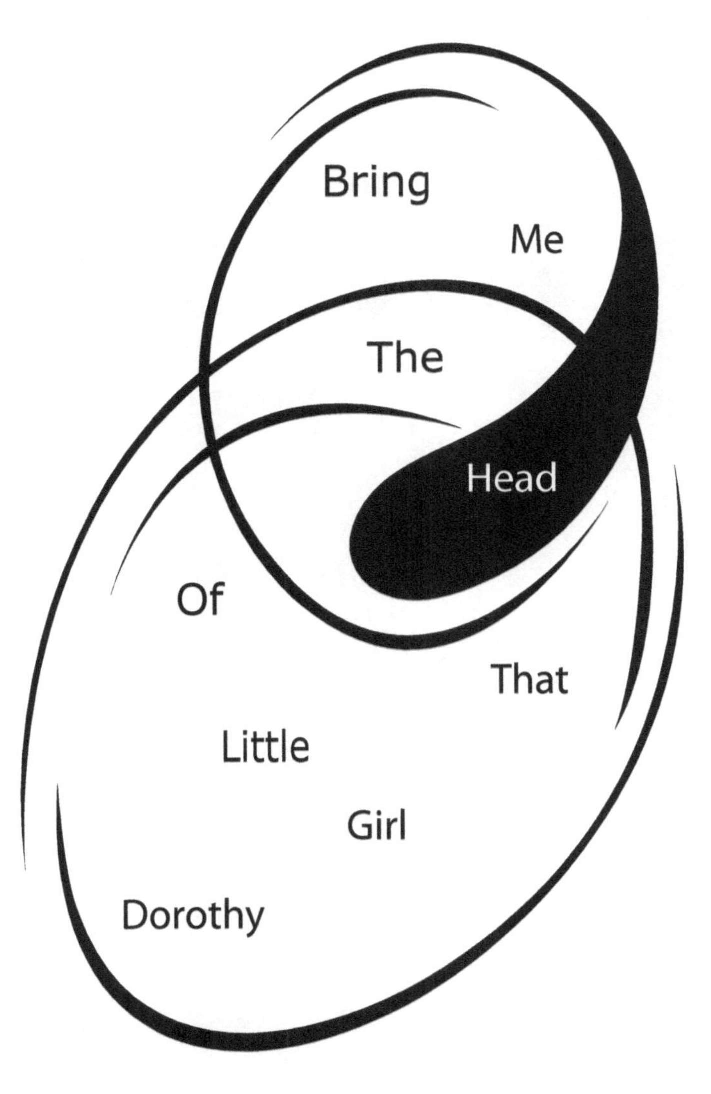

Bring
Me
The
Head
Of
That
Little
Girl
Dorothy

When the Witch calls for Nikko, it's never a good sign.

In the Baum book, the Flying Monkeys were compelled to follow the Witch's orders by the power of the Golden Cap, which could be used only three times by its wearer. I should be so lucky. Three times and out would have saved us all a lot of blood and tears.

In reality, there never was a Golden Cap. The Flying Monkeys are no more coerced into the Witch's service than her Winkie guards. Long ago, choices were made. Bargains struck. Desires fulfilled. Bonds forged. We do our work of our own free will. Regrets, though a burden, do not inform our actions. We are mostly happy monkeys. Violent and stupid, but happy.

There's hardly any real wickedness in the books. Some might say the same about our Land. Those who wouldn't, can't, anymore.

That's my job.

As King of the Flying Monkeys, the burden of regret falls most heavily on me. As does the responsibility for fulfilling our bargain with the Witch. It is Nikko the witch calls for when she wants her Flying Monkeys to attack; Nikko who leads them to their victims, looks back on the bodies broken by his tribe, and sheds a gentle shower of tears. It is with Nikko that the Witch shares her troubles, jealousies, rages, petty frustrations and pompous ambitions. Nikko is her most intimate confidant, the most trusted of lieutenants, the one who stands by her side as she peers into her crystal ball, and the one who is left, even now, alone to whisper into the ears of her many captive heads, and cackle.

I am the creature who satisfies her every wish and desire.

Some say it is the fur that stokes her lust, and others the wings, but I know from experience how much she likes tails. And, of course, there is always the frenzy of a Flying Monkey unleashed, and the way blood drips from a paw when the fury subsides, to spark a dying fire back to life.

Service to the Witch has its rewards. As king of the Flying Monkeys, and as bearer of our guilt, those pleasures also fall mostly on me.

The Witch has summoned her Nikko. The Flying Monkeys screech from their towers, knowing I will lead them soon, again.

It is not a good sign for whoever has angered the Witch.

*

In this *dream* of a *real world*, I work as a design consultant for a large and famous marketing firm with an enormous stick up its ass.

"Maribel," they ask, "which do you think works better?" as they hold up wedges of the color they call lemon so subtly different in value it would take powers of perception both superhuman and from another planet to tell them apart. But the palette under consideration at this meeting has been cleared by the legal department against infringement on competitive product colors, and the team is desperate to come up with the 'new avocado,' and they know through grim experience what'll happen if they don't get my "input," so I have to make a decision based on my years of immersion in the tastes and fashions of this so-called real world, my grasp on the hungers and desires of the consumer masses, and the statistically proven color preferences for particular products by our target demographic.

Fuck the lemon. I want to blow them all to hell.

Let me just say that Maribel is tired. S h e ' s been what passes for "stable" for many years, but she's starting to go crazy, again. It's the Wizard's fault. He won't let her be who she is, where she belongs. He even has her talking to herself in the third person when things get rough. Because it's safer.

Usually she talks to the ceramic monkey.

But I'm tired of playing it safe trying to juggle realities and dreams. I'm sick of being pulled out of where I want to be by a psychic bungee cord.

Those are the rules, I was told.

I made choices. I could have gone back to see the Wizard on my own, demanded he grant my wish to stay. But I was always afraid. He has that effect. Instead, I followed the rules. Made commitments. For a long while, I juggled.

But you can't fight reality. Not all of them. Not for long. They come back to bite you in the ass, sometimes while you're sleeping, or sipping a single-malt and watching the city's lights through your floor-to-ceiling condo window, but these days just as often in the back of a taxi talking on a cell phone or at a business lunch at the latest trendy Soho bistro or even in the middle of a multi-media presentation to a room full of account executives.

I'm going to have to make a move soon. But there are risks. What if I'm just psychotic. Or very neurotic. I might wind up in a hospital again with a doctor pumping me full of drugs, which would only cover the wreckage of what goes on inside me under a sea of very smooth, uniform and hard concrete.

I've been there. That's not any reality.

But if I have to look at one more wedge of lemon, I might start dumping water on people to see if they melt.

*

Slippers, whether silver or ruby, have never mattered to the Witch. She had as many slippers as former rivals, entire halls filled with magical trinkets and memorabilia: a belt of severed arms; serpent clippings from an old skull too dangerous to keep on display; a weathered bow and a quiver of arrows. There was even an empty trunk carved with unknown runes, reserved for the artifacts of her mother's life, if she'd had one.

It's always been about the heads.

"Chop off the head, and the body will soon follow," the Witch is always fond of saying.

If the Witch had her way, there would be nothing but headless bodies walking around, keeping the Land just the way she likes it. More than once, I've caught her staring at my neck in dawn's half-light, when she thought I'd fallen asleep in her lap.

The heads ring the walls of her bedchamber, at the top of her personal tower, above the anteroom which houses her crystal ball. They're always watching, and they never blink. They hear everything that goes on. But these days, they rarely speak. Their mouths are stuffed with garlic, which she removes only when a dire strategical problem forces her to consult an old enemy who may hold a clue to its resolution. As a reward for cooperating, the chosen head is bathed and groomed, taken to a catacomb filled with music boxes and allowed an hour to listen to a chorus of mechanical voices of their choosing. For punishment, an unresponsive head is given to the Flying Monkeys for our sport, hurled through the air, smashed to the ground and against the rock walls at the foundations of the Witch's castle, until there is nothing left of flesh, bone or hair.

As a token of her esteem, the Witch elevated the head of my old Queen when she accepted my allegiance, so that I would have a familiar face to talk to. But the heads of Flying Monkeys fail to remain animated in this Land. Or even preserved.

So it wasn't the slippers the Witch was after when she called for old Nikko.

The Witch had heard the whispers. Of course. Even the monkeys knew what had happened.

Whirlwinds and falling houses were not completely unknown in the Land. But a town's populace spontaneously breaking out into song and dance was another matter, entirely. And news of citizen columns hitting the road seeking brains, hearts and courage, and worse, daring to demand wishes granted from the Wizard, was as chilling as any bombastic threat or pastoral poem that ever emerged from the Emerald City.

A new enemy had come to trouble the Land, and the Witch didn't care about her own shadow, which she'd sent to investigate the weather disturbances; or the slippers this new arrival had stolen from that shadow of the Witch she killed on her arrival; or the little dog of a familiar she'd brought along for a companion; or where she'd come from or where she was heading.

Dorothy, people called the stranger, and the only thing that was on the Witch's mind when she called me to her bedchamber was stopping the revolution before it had a chance to start.

"Bring me the head of that little girl Dorothy," the Witch said.

And then she whispered a few things in my ear, and my cap and jacket fell off, and my tail wandered as if with a will of its own, and the girl Dorothy was allowed to keep her head a while longer while the Witch found solace and comfort and quivering pleasure in the furry embrace of my arms, legs and tail.

But soon enough I was unleashed on the crest of the Witch's true fury, and I called out my brethren and we flew off to find this Dorothy and satisfy my Witch's need.

*

"She's too old," I sense them saying in their private little IM's to each other. "She doesn't have a clue about what the kids want," I read on their lips, a useful if sometimes depressing skill for the corporate office wars. Or, my favorite, "She's not all there," overheard as I sit with my feet up in bathroom stalls.

I never was, honey.

I was born over the rainbow, half-way between a dark place and a light one. Maybe most of us are.

But for me, that dark place was alive, rich and thick like milk I could swim in and drink. That's where I liked to stay. But half the time I wound up in the light, which for all its sound and fury really came across faint and ghostly, as if I was sipping that life through a very narrow straw. The dark spoiled me with its infinitely deep and perpetually sudden presence. I cried when I was thrust back in the light. I was always hungry for more.

Mommy said I was a cranky baby.

The dark left me in peace, but the light was always teaching me things about the solidity of things and the intangibility of sound, the connection between action and consequence, the sequence of old and new. Past, present, future.

Words.

They came to me in the stories and poems I heard, the television shows I watched. Words shaped the world of light, and in its reflection, the dark. Except that, because they were made from the dark, what came to be from the dark made everything in the light seem like a shadow.

I liked the dark even more.

I wasn't an easy child. My older brothers said I was born retarded. Day care workers and teachers said I had an over-active imagination. Dad stopped talking to me. Mom took me to a child psychologist.

I don't know why. I was getting all the help I needed.

In the reality that was the dark of a dream, a woman who said she was my sister came to me, all glittery and full of light that was really just shimmering darkness. Being around her tickled me outside and in, and her cinnamon and apple smell filled my mouth with sweetness and made my belly full. And she could do the most amazing things, like fly through the air, and talk to the trees and the flowers and even the animals. She knew the names of all the new things popping up in the real world growing out of darkness, and introduced me around, and showed me how to do a few tricks just like her.

She didn't explain everything. I'd noticed how the dark caught the reflections of things in the light, so I asked where my mother was, and how she could be my sister when I only had brothers in the light. But instead of answering, she said it was more important for me to understand about being born between worlds, and how I had to work hard at keeping them separate by juggling reality and dream in my head, or else I'd wind up being nowhere and everything would be gone.

She said I had to play a game, only there was no winning or losing. The point was to keep playing the game so I could get stronger and smarter for when I returned to my reality. I listened to the rules she said I had to follow, and I played the game the way she wanted me to in my dream. It was something different to do, and it made the time go by faster in the light while I waited to go back to the other place born from the dark.

For a while.

It was fun to pretend to be a little girl going to school, doing homework, eating dinner with her family, fighting with her brothers, giggling with her friends. Dad talked to me, again, and Mommy stopped taking me to the psychologist. But there wasn't enough excitement.

To keep my interest in the game, I watched the shapes lips made when speaking, so I'd know if my parents were talking about me when they took me to the park and let me run further off than usual, or what my friends were really saying about me when I came up on them in school. I used the secrets I learned in the tricks I played, which were fun, and which I thought would make me strong. Pretty soon I could set fights off between my brothers, parents, friends and enemies.

It was a different kind of fun. Dangerous. Almost like magic.

But not quite. I got hurt, too. A teacher caught me and called me a little witch. Kids would watch me and then beat me up. And I couldn't do magic to protect myself, or make up new friends to replace the broken ones.

The game stopped being fun. I wanted to spend all my time in the reality of my dream, and stop pretending to be someone I wasn't.

I thought hard about the problem, and found only one solution. I tried killing that phoney person.

What a mistake that was.

Before I knew what happened, my reality was sealed up behind a concrete wall of medication. The dream became everything, and even that was foggy. I don't remember much from that time, except that I wasn't in either place I'd been born between.

The doctors eased up on the medication after my parents complained I'd turned into a zombie. My brothers had a good time with that one. But the reality of my dream showed up, and my sister warned me I'd lose the world I'd been trying to get to if I tried anything stupid like that again.

To make her point, she took me to see the Wizard in a place called the Emerald City, where people sang and danced and ate ice cream all day without getting sick. He was nothing more than a shimmering curtain of a face floating in a huge shiny room with lots of echoes, but he didn't feel like a part of the dark that had become my own reality. So right from the start, I was afraid of him. Then the Wizard said, with all his sound and fury:

THAT'S NOT THE WAY THINGS ARE DONE.

And his rolling thunder of a voice knocked me almost all the way back to the dream of a reality.

He had a few other things to say, but my ears hurt when he talked and his voice filled my head with noise. Never mind the terror. His advice was hard to sort out. At least at first.

But I listened. Didn't have a choice. He scared me good. I forgot all about asking him for something, like I'd heard you were supposed to. I believed I'd lose the real world, where I was free to do what I pleased, if I tried to get out of the dream where I couldn't do anything. So I learned some more about juggling.

In the dream, an art therapist introduced me to painting, and suddenly I felt like my older, glittery sister: I could make something real and true that no one else could. It was like learning magic in the light. I did my best early or late in the day, when the sun made common things like abandoned cars, construction machinery, trash bins, all so beautiful. You're doing it right, Mom said, with tears in her eyes. Even Dad would stare. My treatment team agreed I had a vision and talent.

The therapist laughed when I told her about my other place and the sister I had there. You just keep juggling, she told me, like your sister told you to. And don't mention your imaginary sister to the doctors.

I didn't argue the imaginary point.

My sister did her part, sending me to stay with aunts in dark forests, and mountain tops, and damp caves by the sea where I met odd and smelly women who taught me tricks with words and numbers, steel and straw, fire and water. I learned all about the secret workings of the real place I lived in, and soon enough I knew the names of all the things I saw, understood the depths and subtleties of the making of things, and their unmaking. I could count to seventeen by two's both forward and backward and make things happen the way I wanted them to, most of the time. More often than anyone else, anyway.

But no one ever explained how I could spend so much time in one place, and have it seem that only moments had passed when I found myself having returned to the other. It was another mystery, like having a sister in my real world, but no Mom or Dad, or bunch of brothers. It was like the Wizard, and how he could be the only thing I was afraid of in the place I wanted to live.

I once asked my mother if she'd been taking drugs when she was carrying me, or if there was a family disease or an ancient curse passed from one generation to the next that I needed to know about, or if anything unusual happened during her pregnancy, like an alien abduction, or a visit from Peter Pan.

She said no, I was the only crazy one in the family.

When I asked Dad if I might have inherited anything from his side of the family, he took me out hunting with my brothers, to teach me what the real world was all about and get closer to my own kin, so I could act more normal.

He stopped when he was tired of my misses and the accidents I always seemed to cause, though I could track as well as they could, and shoot better than any of them.

I asked my sister where she came from, and all the new things in my reality, since when I was born there'd only been the dark and I hadn't known how to make things back then.

She said she and I and everything else came from where all things come from, and where all things go back to once they're done here, and there was no point looking too close at that place because I might fall in and then everything would be gone, and here's another trick I didn't know that she could teach me, if only I paid attention.

Nobody ever gives anyone a straight answer.

Except for the Wizard.

Maybe that's why I've put off going to him for so long. And why my best friend in this dream is a ceramic monkey.

*

We ate the dog.

We are Flying Monkeys, after all, and you can't blame us. The animal was in a picnic basket. The worst we thought we were doing was eating Dorothy's lunch. After all, she wasn't going to need it.

Then we went after the girl. Her friends put up a fight. A good one. I lost few subjects. But I won the trophy of a metal arm, and tasted with the sweet straw taste of victory.

We took Dorothy's head. Ripped it right off her body.

And that's when things really went bad.

*

Somewhere in the past, between dropping the painting and taking up the gospel word of the holy consumer, I took on a husband and popped out a couple of kids. What the hell was I thinking?

Don't fight the dream, join it, that's what.

Honestly. Can you imagine? I thought flesh and blood, things and money, could anchor me to this dream. Make it real.

As if.

The artsy life went first. Nobody cared about my little realities. But I was strangely suited to advertising and a corporate life. Go figure. Like all the bullshit you have to go through kissing and kicking ass was enough to make me believe the other place was a lie and that I had a place in this world.

Problem was, I kept getting pulled back to that reality. Hard to kick a habit sweeter than any drug when that habit shoots itself into you at random. Never mind being born with that more-real-than-reality world flowing through the veins.

Family was my last honest shot. I thought I could huddle with a hubby around the midnight fire of our old age.

I can almost hear the Wizard: THAT'S NOT THE WAY THINGS ARE DONE.

My ex actually cried when I agreed he should leave, and take the kids, because I wasn't, as he put it, "participating in our family life, much less being the mother to our son and daughter." He was a good man. We had some fun, in that dreamy way that never touched my heart.

They're better off without me.

I still look out for my kids in my reality, just in case they inherited a latent gene from me, or they get used by an up and coming enemy. Hate to chop off my own kids' heads. Especially after all the trouble I went through giving birth to them.

Just goes to show I'm not all bad, and even quite human, in this dream of a reality. For whatever that's worth.

*

The thing about heads is that they never shut up. Separated from their bodies, it's as if their minds and tongues have been liberated. Without bodies, brains feel no shame in endless banter, in expressing every little random thought. It's really quite rude.

Sorry, but that's the truth.

Monkeys don't have that problem. Even we Flying Monkeys don't talk when head and body are separated. We don't talk much, anyway, except for myself. As their King, it's my duty to negotiate for what is best for my people within the terms of our bargain with the Witch. These are delicate matters, and though the Witch confides in me with a certain level of trust, I must be as eloquent as I am passionate in my appeals.

Mostly, we screech before the blade cuts our vocal chords. After that, we're quiet. We screech when we launch ourselves into the air for an attack, and when we begin our actual assault, and in the heat of battle, and when we return to our towers with the spoils of our victory. We also screech when the Witch clips our wings. We are quiet when we make love, and when we eat, and even when our females deliver our young. We offer no lullabies to our infants, no sweet stories of a never-land or a sweet future. When our young turn on us, and eat us so they can take our place, we do not beg or plead, scream or reason. In the service of the Witch, there are neither idle nor desperate conversations about past or future. There is only now.

We do not want to lose our wings. They are our only freedom.

The heads in the Witch's bedchamber can't control themselves. I was the one who advised stuffing their mouths with garlic and sealing their lips behind silk scarves. I found their chatter distracting, though the Witch didn't seem to mind. I think she liked the cacophony. As she enjoys our screeching. But if I was expected to offer my sage counsel, I needed to think. She understood. I am, after all, only a Flying Monkey, even if I am a King.

I also wanted them to shut up when I talked.

Is that too much to ask?

Sometimes, I listen to one or two when she's not around, or not all there. Just to see if I can pick something useful out of the babble.

I also occasionally get drawn into a conversation with a head I'm carrying back to the Witch.

I do that, sometimes, when the flight is long and I'm tired of listening to the noise my people make, and I want to learn more about the Witch's enemies so I might protect and serve her more effectively.

There's also idle curiosity. I am still a monkey, after all.

Heads don't need prompting. When they're done wailing, whining, and asking stupid questions about what has and will happen to them, they settle into their own little worlds and never get out. It's all about them. What they did, who they were, on and on. I just ask the questions that get them to the parts of their lives I find interesting.

But Dorothy didn't wail or whine. She didn't ask stupid questions. And she never talked about herself. She did ask me questions people don't usually ask monkeys, flying or otherwise, like: where did I come from, what did I want, and, who was I?

Had I ever gone to see the Wizard?

I knew I wasn't in the Witch's company, anymore.

*

"Maribel, have you gone crazy?" the Human Resources Administrator asked. A representative from the legal department sat by her side as she sifted through print outs of the records on her screen.

"Not yet," I replied. And I was being quite sincere. There weren't any bodies, yet. I'd just been letting off a little steam. Firing a few warning shots across the bow. Ringing the bells and sounding the horns that warn passing ships they stray too close to dangerous shores.

The monitors were due to be replaced next year, anyway. And Jack's coffee maker made too much noise. How could anyone get any work done?

Frankly, Denise had it coming, and I don't think the HR Administrator would find anyone on the floor who'd back her side of the story, even if it was true.

And the other incidents haven't even reached HR yet.

Who did these people think they were, the Wizard?

Of course, they had no idea of what I'm capable of doing. In the reality of my dream, I take no shit. None. The people there found that out when I got tired of my sister's line of bullshit.

I cornered her in the castle one day. If I have parents in the place that's a dream, I asked her, why don't I have parents here? Who's your mother? Why isn't she mine, if you're my sister? How can I have aunts without a mother? Is she dead? Banished? Is the Wizard keeping her prisoner in the Emerald City? Is the Wizard my mother?

And then I got serious:

Who the hell are you? Where did you come from? What do you want from me?

Are you a spy for the Wizard?

The questions upset her. She shed glitter like dandruff, and looked like water might melt her, after all. I blew off her old tricks of farming me off to another aunt or distracting me with the secret of another spell. Then she tried this chestnut: the Wizard already explained everything to me, so I should know better than to ask silly questions. I should concentrate on rising to the responsibilities of my station in this world instead of losing myself in nonsense.

Come on. Who did she think she was, the Wizard?

I wasn't even sure she was my sister. She didn't look like me, and she didn't have to handle being in two places. Could she even understand what I was going through trying to stay sane while bouncing back and forth between two very different worlds with hardly any say in the matter, no matter what kind of medication I took, no matter how many spells I learned?

She told me I shouldn't ask so many questions, because sometimes answers are more troubling than the problems that provoked the questions. Then she started in on how I shouldn't show off my powers to the common people, and that I should concentrate on doing good deeds and helping others. I was a good girl, in a good place, and I had to do everything in my power to keep what I had nice and clean and good.

I actually flinched when she said that last word a third time. By the fourth, it felt like a magic stake shoved through my heart.

I told her I wasn't in this reality to do good deeds. This was my world. I'd made it.

And when I said that, the truth of my reality hit me: I was the mommy. My sister, my aunts, all the Land and everything in it, were things I'd made out of the dark, in the shapes of things I'd seen and heard about in the light. Whether I'd been in control or not when I made these things didn't matter. The magic was here to amuse me, and whatever I did with it was just fine.

When I told her that one, I thought my sister was going to have a heart attack right there. She raised her hand to me.

Actually.

Raised.

Her.

Hand.

Juggle this, bitch.

She was the first head in my collection.

For a minute, I was thinking maybe this human resource administrator was going to be the latest.

But, of course, that would have been wrong. Say whatever else you want about me, I can tell where I am and what's appropriate behavior in that place. I've had practice juggling.

"We can advise counseling," the Administrator said. "The clinic our company health insurance uses is also covered through your personal insurance. We checked. We don't want to lose you. You've been with us for so long, as an employee and consultant. You're part of the family."

I heard the 'you old bitch,' even if the words were never spoken. "You just want to medicate me," I said.

"If the doctors recommend it, yes, we'd have to insist you remain in whatever treatment you entered until you were cleared to return to work."

"I've tried the meds. They don't work. The dream of reality doesn't go away. And neither does the reality of the dream."

The HR person was good. She never blinked or made a funny, puzzled face. "Sometimes you have to make those choices yourself, Maribel. Drugs can't make them for you."

"I understand. I think I've made my choice."

The company gave me a decent buy out of my consulting contract. No one wanted a scandal to reach the free-agent circuit or float through the trades.

I sold the condo and everything in it, took the cash and hit the road. It was time to go pay a visit to the one person I was still afraid of, the creature I'm sure I never made. It was time to see the Wizard.

Sometimes, you just have to get your wish granted.

*

Sometimes, the Witch isn't here, even when she is.

She eats, sleeps, and flies around on her broom well enough. Her eyes track motion, she answers questions and gives orders. But she doesn't smell the same. The sweet pastry scent with a hint of cinnamon and nutmeg is gone. And when I lick her, she tastes like sand instead of brown sugar. She never yells or screams, and her punishments are unimaginative: the old draw-and-quartering, common stoning, or the dull stand-by, thrown to the hungry tigers.

During those times, I'm just another monkey, not Nikko, her pet King, her most intimate companion. Those are lonely times for old Nikko.

When I ask if anything is wrong, she says no. I mention the Wizard, and she ignores me. You'd think keen animal senses could detect her comings and goings, and even follow her to where she goes when she leaves us. But I've never been able to track her, even when she empties out while I'm sitting on her lap. Often, I only find out she's back when the castle smells like a bakery, or when I ask her how she feels and she grabs me by the tail and swings me through the air, smashing me into a wall or throwing me through a window. Sometimes, when she returns from wherever she went lost in thought, she'll satisfy herself by hurling a random head or two in my direction.

Once she nearly pulled my wings off. That was

when I suggested she declare a truce with the Wizard and see if he could come up with a cure for her condition.

She was there when I came back with Dorothy's head. All there. More there than ever.

Heat came off her body like steam, singeing a few of my hairs and making me dance like an organ grinder's lackey. Her eyes went deep, like their depths had sunk another thousand fathoms through layers of primordial debris to sound the true bottom of her terror, to make way for a new expanse of wonder at what lay before her.

And her voice, when she finally spoke, was as loud as the Wizard's when it booms from the Emerald City during one of his rages, as powerful as the whirlwinds that brings visitors from far places, and as fragile as the shell that protects this world from all those other places, near and far.

She was there in her fullest glory, as if she knew I'd spoken with Dorothy's head and wanted me to understand that she felt betrayed.

I knew I was in trouble even before I landed in her highest chamber: the cold head I'd been carrying suddenly became hot, and a familiar scent of cinnamon rose from the head's limp hair.

The Witch found out. She must have been watching me in her crystal ball. I didn't know Dorothy, or the troubling questions she asked, were that important.

I was only trying to help my Witch.

The depth of her rage was something new and terrible, and even my monkey sense couldn't get to the bottom of the fear that fed it. I worried over what I had brought to her, and what might happen to me, to us, to my people and this land. I would have let the head slip away and claimed I lost it, or said it had been ruined by a stray blow from the woodsman accompanying her, doing damage she couldn't see in her crystal ball, if I'd known the terrible consequence of fulfilling my duties.

For a dark moment, I thought of flying off and leaving them alone with each other. After all, if she really was in a jealous rage, she might want to rip my wings off and toss me from her tower. Or worse. But I never let go of the Witch.

I am her King, and I understood what I had to do. I thought I could help.

I never let her go.

Instead, I came before her bearing the head of the little girl Dorothy, and I asked that the Witch grant her a reprieve. I thought she'd been very forthcoming on the flight to the Witch's castle. And her passion for truth burned with the intensity of a false witch on one of my Witch's pyres. I could see why the populace had embraced her, and why the Witch considered her so dangerous. Still, the Witch might learn something from her.

"Take her to the tower," the Witch said. Her voice scattered my people and nearly made me drop the head. I fell to my knees, cap blown off, vest torn to tatters. My wings shriveled.

"She isn't one of your usual enemies," I said, and to my ears I wasn't even screeching, merely squealing. "She may not even be an enemy at all."

"Is that all you learned from your intimate little conversation?" the Witch asked. Her thundering voice was streaked with suspicion, as if I'd broken our treaty and changed my allegiance. I shivered. "The Wizard sent her to kill me."

"She never saw the Wizard," I said, and it took all of my courage, brains and heart. "She was only on the road to see him. She doesn't even know who you are. She's not from around here. All she ever talks about is going home." I'd heard she could read lips, so I never lied to the Witch. But I also knew it would have been hard to read Dorothy's lips, since I hold heads close to me so they won't fall out of my hands.

"She *is* home." The way the Witch towered over me suggested I'd lost mine.

"Yes. Quite so. But she came from someplace else, and judging from my conversation with her, I suspect there are more young girls just like her waiting to follow." The Witch didn't like that possibility. I pressed my point. "She obviously has power, but do you know what it is? Can you use it? Can you even take it away from her? And what if she was sent to kill you by some other enemy outside the Land, set to invade our quiet corner. Shouldn't you find out all you can about this enemy, his strength and his plans?" I waited, because sometimes it pays to hesitate, before the final drive to the heart of the matter. And then I said, "Shouldn't you use whatever comes to you to strike first?"

I could hear her heart quicken at the possibility of a threat. Her eyelids fluttered, her habit when calculating the risk of extending herself beyond the limits of her realm, or considering a final assault on the Wizard, or doing anything else she is too afraid to do.

For so many years, she's held back.

"You are wise, little monkey. I feel in my bones that there is more here than meets the eye."

"You are too gracious, my Witch."

"Yes, I am. I will speak with the head of this Dorothy."

"By your will."

Sometimes, it's like pulling off your own wings.

*

It's lonely on the road, in the dream of this reality. Even with a ceramic monkey for company.

When I drive late into the night, the beams of my head lights turns the highway to gold and I think I really am in that other place, on the road to the Emerald City and the Wizard.

But then dawn breaks, or I hit a bright city, and I snap back into the a world where there is no Wizard, only the slowly shrinking pile of money that keeps me going on the road.

In the cheap motel beds where I lay like a speared whale on the deck of a ship sent to gut me, I feel my kids shift and kick as if they were still inside me. My back aches from the memory of their weight. The fresh-flesh smell of their hair and skin, the soft smoothness of their warm, wiggling little bodies under my fingers, their gurgling when I changed their diapers, the heat when I held them to my heart, come back to me like a song, filling every empty space I have in this world. But only for the flicker of a moment.

They're only part of the dream, not the reality where I live.

One of the things I remember the Wizard telling me, after the ringing of his first pronouncement faded away, was that I should never trust the Land. Or myself in the Land. My sister said the same thing. It's just a dream, they said. That's how we can have no mother or father. Without you out there in the real world, we'd all die.

But I thought they were trying to trick me. I figured they were jealous because I could do whatever I wanted to and because so many people in the Land liked me. I was stronger, and smarter, than my sister, and even the Wizard, even if I couldn't stay in the reality of my dream all the time. The Wizard and my sister wanted to control me, just like all the teachers and bullies, doctors and nurses, my parents and brothers.

That's when I came to understand I was my own mother, and I killed my sister and made sure the Wizard never had any ideas about leaving his little Emerald City to rouse the countryside rabble.

And yet, after all the loneliness of this road I'm on, I see now that they may have had a point. I've had time to think. Frankly, my reality is occasionally a little too strange.

There are Flying Monkeys and talking heads. Being my own mother raises certain metaphysical questions I'm not prepared to answer – and how happy my sister would be to hear that admission. I'm loved, but I feel awfully alone.

I finally remembered what everyone calls me, even my friends:

Witch.

I'm not quite at the point where I wish I was back trying to tell the difference between two swatches of lemon yellow. But I can see the attraction in that level of the mundane. There's a certain relief in not experiencing all aspects of reality in a high-octane *now*. There's an excitement to anticipating something that will happen in the future, and mellow joy in looking back at the past.

Maybe the Land doesn't ring as true as it once did because I have nothing concrete to come back to, just a car, or a motel room that looks exactly like all the others I've slept in, or a diner or fast food restaurant or gas station bathroom. I should have allowed myself to be destitute and homeless long ago, instead of grounding myself in material things.

Maybe this dream's infected me with its banality.

I've gone back to painting. I look for the light in the morning, and at sunset. I tried to do landscapes, then portraits, and finally threw myself into surreal, abstract, conceptual, whatever chapter from the art history books I happened upon on a particular day. Everything I tried to do came out looking like the something out of my other life.

I ride the road because that's how you get to see the Wizard. You have to follow the road, whatever color the brick may be.

But I'm not reaching the Wizard. I'm not even trying, in the other place, as far as I can tell. And here, I'm not doing too well, either. It's hard to remember why I'm even looking for the Wizard, much less who he might be, and where.

What would I ask of him?

With the money dribbling away like blood from a wound that won't heal, I've had to do a little tutoring, sales, waiting tables, inventory, even a window display for a Chicago department store.

Yesterday, I got another waitress job at a truck stop in Kansas.

And here, deep in the fields of poppy in which I've lost myself, listening to the truckers and the local kids and the ones just traveling through on the old Santa Fe trail, heading west or east to a promised land of plenty or maybe just home, a little rat voice nibbled at me with sharp-edged words of desperation between orders of steak and eggs or steak and fries and more black coffee.

"She's awful quiet in there," said a man.

Those words made me remember that I really did want to leave this dream of a reality. And why. Suddenly, I was who I am, both in this realm and in my reality. I remembered what I wanted from the Wizard.

And because THAT'S NOT THE WAY THINGS ARE DONE, like the Wizard said, I had to do something about what I found out. I knew if I did, I'd find the the directions I needed to take on the road to see the Wizard.

It felt good to be the Witch and Maribel at the same time.

Everything would turn out just fine.

*

In my position as King of the Flying Monkeys, I sat in the window of the Witch's bedchamber while she spoke with Dorothy's head.

The Chief Winkie – he likes to call himself Flip – stood in the door holding his ridiculous lance straight up like the monkey hard-on he wished he had. If that thing wouldn't stop him from rushing in to save the Witch if she was in trouble, his stupid runaway beaver dam of a hat would.

I, on the other hand, was ready as always to put my body between danger and my Witch, or leap out and lead my people to war against whatever invaders Dorothy represented.

I like to think my presence gave the Witch a measure of added confidence, even if she didn't allow me time to find myself a new hat and vest. A small measure, granted, being all-powerful and almost all-knowing, but a measure, nonetheless.

"Look what the twisters dragged in," said the Witch, in her favorite high-pitched, tremulous whine she reserved for intimidating strangers.

"Took them long enough," Dorothy said. "I've been waiting for a ride all my life, and even if I am a figment of your imagination, that's still a mighty long time–"

"Stop rambling," the Witch said, with a slight frown. "And don't play with me. I didn't make you. You're from the outside. Where?"

"The politically correct answer is Kansas, which poses no threat to you, I can assure you, and I'm supposed to say all I'm trying to do is to go home –"

"Of course. Now that you've spread your lies though the populace and turned them against me, hired your spies and signed your secret pacts with the Munchkins, it's time for you to return to your secret masters and tell them my land is ripe for invasion!"

"– but of course all that's as corny as Kansas, if you'll pardon the expression, because you and I know that everything here is just a figment of your imagination, and you don't let anything in, except for the Wizard, who's not so much a stranger as the place where a stranger might occupy if you actually let anyone this deep into your warped little world –"

"Lies and obfuscations," the Witch said, losing her whine and beginning to thunder, which was usually a sign for me to start flapping my wings. I stood fast, hoping Dorothy would break through like she did with me. The Witch really needed to hear what I had if she was planning to get anywhere in life, and take us both where she was supposed to be.

"Not at all. I'm just a little piece of our self gone out looking for the rest of us, so we can drag the whole gang of us back to the real world and look for our husband and kids. You know, they need you. And you need them."

The kids did the trick. A little flame went on in the Witch's eyes. I knew Dorothy hadn't been lying. The Witch had a whole other life away from us. That's where she went, when she wasn't with us.

She had another land, a real family. A husband who was her king.

Maybe it was a place where she'd be happier. After all, I'm only a monkey. Still, there might be a place for me at her side.

"You're saying you're me?"

"Hell no. I see you're too used to giving orders in here to listen. Pay attention: I'm just one little bitty piece of you. Like dandruff. A poor little need you shed so fast it never sparked into a desire, never surfaced into a thought. You've got pieces scattered all over the place. Buried a few. Your court is filled with identity fragments, but, of course, they're the more obvious kinds of things you hunger for."

"What a novel conceit. You say you're a part of me yet look nothing like me. Are you another sister? A daughter born out of me in my sleep by a miracle?"

"Honey, it's all pretty miraculous down here, in case you haven't noticed. You don't have to look much past you and the monkey to figure that out. So don't worry about it. Just roll with the punches and come back. Over the rainbow. To where the rest of you is looking for the part she's missing."

"Don't you want to go back?"

"I can't. Not until you do. Then we all get back."

"You want me to fly over the rainbow to another land, where your people can ambush and attack me and then invade my land."

"Take it easy. Nobody wants to attack anyone. People just want to talk. Relate. Connect. And that most heinous of crimes: bond."

"No one binds the Witch."

"Exactly."

"Time to put you up on a shelf, dear Dorothy. Your attempted insurgency is over. I'm afraid you've not proven as amusing as Nikko said you might be."

The Witch gave me one of those looks that always made my hair stand on end and my balls freeze. The Winkie snickered.

But Dorothy came through. Before the Witch could plug her mouth, the kid asked, "What are you afraid of?"

Most people never ask the question because the answer seems obvious, and if there is something she's afraid of, nobody wants to know what that might be.

"Nothing," the Witch said. But she'd stopped dead in her tracks to consider.

"Really. So you keep a standing army of Winkies and Flying Monkeys, practice terminal spell craft and live in a castle even though no one has ever posed a serious threat to you. Not even once." Dorothy's eyes rolled.

The Witch opened her mouth, and I scanned the heads in the chamber, knowing she considered quite a few of them serious. But maybe, like Dorothy said, they were all just pieces of herself she'd conquered. Some of them were quite nice. A few even liked me for what I was.

"There's always the Wizard," I said, playing my part to keep things going. I gambled on the Witch being too distracted by Dorothy to do anything but give me another look, which she did.

Your balls get numb after a while.

"Okay," Dorothy said, and you could tell she was trying to nod her head but had forgotten she no longer had a neck to nod with. "He's the problem we're going to have to get past if we're going to get all of our selves together. So let's go see this Wizard and blow this joint."

A deep shadow settled over the Witch's face. "Are you saying the Wizard orchestrated this deceit?"

"If that's what it'll take to get you moving, then yes, the Wizard is the man behind the curtain manipulating us all."

The Witch turned to show me her disappointment, hurt and contempt, as if I'd failed her by missing such an obvious ploy.

She looked out one of her windows, but didn't set me lose on Dorothy, didn't order me to attack the Emerald City and drag the Wizard back to her. Instead, she said, "This time he's gone too far. It's time we've settled who's in charge, once and for all."

"That's my Witch talking. Now let's get going -- you know the way, don't you? Just follow the yellow brick road."

*

They were going to take the girl out to a ghost town and have their fun there.

The three boys looked me over hard to see if I'd overheard, if maybe they should take me along for the ride. I served them like a caterer bringing kosher pigs to a bar mitzvah, joking and flirting like I didn't have a brain in my head, and pretty soon they were back to laughing and flirting right back, treating me like the pathetic, over-the-hill lady I was who'd never find out about that girl they had tied up in the back of their truck, or what they were wanting to do with her. As if I didn't have ears that could pull down gossip at a hundred paces, and eyes that could pick words right off your lips.

Hell, I've been in advertising for thirty years. I'd ruled a whole other world for most of that time. If I couldn't con a bunch of self-absorbed young sociopaths, I'd never have survived my first sales meeting, much less the Wizard.

The Wizard liked things running the way they were supposed to. What they were doing was so wrong, the Wizard himself was bound to show up. Especially if the Witch made an appearance, in the middle of Kansas. That wasn't right. That was definitely not the way things were supposed to be.

Those three boys dragged me right out of my fields of poppy, got me in touch with everyone I was and could be, and set me back on the road to the Wizard. Bless their black little hearts.

I gave them their check, went out the back, stopping by the manager's office to lift that shotgun he kept in the closet, the .38 revolver from his desk, and shells, which he'd shown to me during the interview to let me know he didn't take any crap from the customers. Or the help. I left the automatic and high-powered stuff behind. I didn't want anything to jam.

I took the keys to his SUV, too. Left the last of my signed traveler's checks in exchange, as well as the keys to my own car. I guess I was being optimistic, not leaving my cash, as well.

I was waiting in the SUV when those boys came out, right ahead of the manager and one of the other waitresses, who must have complained about my disappearing. While they were standing around looking at my car like I might have been napping in the back seat, trunk, or maybe underneath, I drove around the lot the other way and followed my boys back on to the highway. I hung back, running without headlights most of the time, racing to catch up when I started losing sight of their lights.

Then the boys went off-road.

I had to turn my lights on, except for when I reached a clearing or went over a rise where we were in clear line of sight of each other. We went on a couple of hours, going fairly straight on the suggestion of a road that wore out completely once we passed a few old, abandoned farms. My bones rattled and my eyes nearly popped out of my head. I held on to the steering wheel with aching hands, bounced along on a bruised ass, until the boys reached a sad little ruin of a town right before dawn. I let my car roll to a stop, then came in on the other side of the cemetery, really just a patch of broken tomb stones, a good half-mile away while they unloaded their truck parked by an old stone building.

There was a chill in the night air as I crept up, slow and quiet, crossing a dried out creek bed and rusty Atchison, Topeka and Santa Fe rails. I wasn't sure if the sound of my engine had carried, but I was hoping those boys would have had their hands full carrying their prize inside.

It felt funny being out under the stars, in the middle of nowhere, with good, honest guns in hand. I wasn't old, anymore. Coming up on those boys was nothing like sitting in a meeting with a bunch of empty suits gnawing over a bone the wrong shade of lemon. And I wasn't bad at it. Even the prairie dogs were surprised. If only those empty suits could see me now.

It brought me back to hunting with my Dad and brothers, and him loving being out in the wilderness. He'd been right. Life's about the hunt. It's about paying attention to everything, living in the moment, in the quiet and the expanse of sky and earth, bonded to place and prey. Almost like being in the dream of my reality.

I was glad I'd picked up a few tricks from him. Dad would have been proud.

Almost made me think about what I'd left behind.

I heard a woman's scream, but I didn't jump in right away. I felt bad, but I told myself I was here for the Wizard, not for her. When it got quiet, I came up to the building. Sure enough, two of the boys were fast asleep near the entrance, and the third one was standing over the girl, pulling his pants back on. She was tied up, but still breathing. He didn't look so young, anymore, and neither did the two on the floor.

I took him out with the shotgun, wheeled around and got the other two while they were scrambling to get up. Then I went around with the pistol and delivered a head shot to each one. The sound of the shotgun was still ringing in my ears, and the .38 sounded like a little dog's bark.

That was Mom. If you're going to do something, she used to say, make sure you do it right.

Skinning them was a temptation. But that would have been too much like the other me. I had to remind myself I wasn't really the Witch, here. I didn't have squadrons of Flying Monkeys and legions of Winkie guards to back me up, much less magical powers. It was enough she was inside me, keeping my nerves steady, my mind focused.

The girl was still alive. I let her go, but on foot, to give me time with the Wizard. He hadn't shown up yet, but he was coming. I could feel it.

She thought I was one of her attackers. I guess the blood all over me didn't help. I had less on me than she did.

I never noticed the blood in the dream of my reality. It was always there. The monkey's fur was full of it after he came back with a head I'd sent him to get. I just never paid it any attention. At first warm, the blood quickly cooled and chilled my skin. Here, it seems like past and future make the blood more real than real.

I was half-asleep in the shadows of one of the out-structures, nothing more than a wooden wall and rubble, with the ceramic monkey wrapped in a sweater in the satchel on my lap, when the Wizard rode in on a motorcycle along a trail of old wagon ruts.

I knew it was him because he had a man's build, not a boy's, like the others, and he walked like he didn't need the gun in his hand to know he was in charge. He didn't take his helmet off when he stopped, and kept the dark face plate down even when he checked out the truck and the stone building before going inside. I came around from the other side, checked him out through one of the windows.

Sure enough, he was waiting by the door,

listening, while standing in a pool of the blood that had leaked from one of the boys. He still hadn't taken his helmet off.

I took him out at the knees, but not before he sensed me at the window and squeezed off a few rounds with his little machine gun.

Bastard.

He isn't the Wizard for nothing.

The echoes of our exchange rang in my ears for a minute. I was too old for this part. The part where the dream hurt. I never liked guns, never fired them after I had to stop tagging along with my Dad and brothers. Certainly never shot at anything that could fire back. All that gunfire and smoke and flash was like being in the Wizard's hall, hearing his booming voice of thunder, and the sudden, vivid memory of that one time I met him shocked me more than the pain in my right side. For a moment, I thought I was back in the dream of my reality, in the Emerald City.

The Witch screamed. She wasn't used to resistance.

I held on to where I really was, to what I'd set out to do. So close. I couldn't let myself down, this close. I crawled through the window, leaving the shotgun behind but keeping the .38 in my good hand and aimed at him. I was losing a lot of blood on the bad side of me, but he was losing more where his legs used to be.

"You killed my friends," he said, his words muffled behind the helmet's visor, as distant as if they'd been piped in from that other place.

"Is this the way things are supposed to be,

you bastard?" I asked, kicking away his gun. He was breathing hard, and his hands were shaking. But he hadn't screamed.

"Who are you, her mother?"

I had to laugh. Even after all this time, there were still questions about mothers. At least I hadn't asked it.

Keeping the gun on him, I flipped the visor up.

Like I almost remembered, he had a beard, and his face was round, like his eyes, and his hair was dark and curly, his skin pitted and scarred. I never thought a wizard could grant so many wishes unscathed.

"We're a little past the mother issue," I said.

The Wizard grunted. "You never get past that one."

I was sure he was toying with me. "So do usually you kill the mothers first and go after the daughters later?"

The Wizard looked around as if searching for another body, then stared at me. I think he was actually scared, not because he was wounded and going into shock while facing his worst enemy, but because he thought that enemy was crazy.

"I guess she's safe, so you got what you came for," he said, then winced. Shivered. He leaned to the side and threw up. When he was finished, he looked up at me and continued with: "We wouldn't have picked her up if we knew you were following her."

I caught myself shaking my head. What was the Wizard talking about? Was that regret I was hearing?

I almost put a bullet in his head. I had to remind myself he was probably delirious.

"You shouldn't have let it go this far," he said. "What the hell kind of mother are you, anyway? Letting us do this much to her, for what? Teach her a lesson? You're a real fucking psychotic, you know that?"

That was more like it. He still didn't understand who I was, but at least he had the attitude of the Wizard I feared.

"That's not the way things are done," I said.

"That's goddam right it isn't." He bowed his head, whimpered, reached for his legs, straightened. "We only pick the runaways. Strays. Nobody misses them." He glanced at his gun. "So are you going to kill me? I didn't touch her."

I shook my head. Maybe this man was like me, tuning in and out of his true reality. But I needed the both of us to be all here, now, for each other. "She wasn't my daughter," I said, trying to ground us in what we really are.

"Then what the hell is all this about?"

"I need you to do something for me."

His expression crinkled into a rumpled sheet of pain, and he lay down on his side. He put his face into the floor, then looked up. "Are you kidding me?"

"No. I've come to see the Wizard so I can get my wish."

"What the hell are you talking about?"

"Don't play games with me. I've known you all my life. People come from far and wide to visit you, to make a wish so their dream can come true. I never stopped them, unless I thought they were a threat to me. I let you play your games, fulfilling hopes or crushing them, according to whatever rules you play by. I never attacked you directly. And yes, I was scared, and I knew I'd want something from you, someday, so yes, I left you alone for selfish reasons. But we both survived. We had our time apart. Now I need something from you. You have to give it to me. Or else I'll go crazy."

I'd lost him. Too many words. He couldn't pay attention, he needed medical attention.

I should have just held him at gunpoint instead of shooting him in the legs. Damn. I didn't know how much I was afraid of him until just then.

His head had drifted back down until his forehead rested against the ground. "You're bug fuck. No clue. I have no clue what you're talking about." He rubbed his thighs, then made a fist. "You want drugs? I didn't bring any. I don't carry them around. So cops can't bust me."

"I don't want drugs," I said. "I want to go back. To the other place. Send me. Make me stay there. Forever. I'm tired of this world, this stupid dream where people are bad, and they do things like this, like what your friends were doing to the girl, and worse."

I expected him to come back with the question, what's the difference? Because then I could say, in the other place, I'm the one who makes all the bad things happen. And if he said it first, then I could say, yes, that's the point.

But instead he said, "I can't send you anywhere." And then he dragged his head up and fixed me with an unsteady gaze, saying, "You're the one sending me to hell."

Suddenly, I knew how the Dorothy from the movie felt when the Wizard said he couldn't get her home.

I aimed for a temple shot, but didn't take it. Not because he winced, or peed in his pants. And certainly not because of our history together in the reality of my dream.

Maybe I didn't finish him because I never wanted to be the Witch in this world.

I walked past him, but without looking, and went out the door. "You're just a kid," I could have said. But I wanted to talk to the Wizard, so instead, I said, "You were going to kill a little girl. That could have been me, twenty five years ago. That could have been Dorothy. If we were in the other place, I'd have my Monkeys drag you out of the Emerald City and cut you up into little parts and have each part sent to every corner of the land so everyone could finally see the Wizard and ask him for what they wanted. I'd do that. I still may."

I headed for my stolen SUV before he had the chance to tell me I was crazy, again. The sun was bright and hot, and my useless right arm itched as if overrun by ants. My blood drew a few flies. The gun was heavy in my good hand and I was questioning whether or not to just drop it at the scene. Maybe I should've searched him for drugs.

There was noise in my head about fingerprints and getting rid of evidence. The part of me that was the Witch was laughing at the concept of an arrest. I was grateful I still had money left.

It wasn't the consequences of theft, or of shooting the Wizard and leaving him in a Kansas ghost town to die, that scared me. It was the possibility of crawling back to my old career, if not my old job, and begging to be allowed to once again make crucial decisions about color palettes for ad campaigns, and dedicating myself to identifying just the right shade that was going to move an extra ten thousand units of a product, that sent cold dread creeping through me like a million year-old glacier.

A familiar mechanical burb erupted behind me just as I was trying to figure out how to get a doctor to patch me up.

Multiple stings jolted me along my back, and my first thought was that I'd disturbed a wasps' nest. Then I fell down.

The ground smacked me hard. Pin pricks of pain swelled up and down my body. At least my bad arm wasn't hurting as badly, in comparison.

Looking back as I lay flat on the earth, so close I could hear the breath of old grudges in the rocks against my ear, I saw the Wizard lying in the doorway of the stone building with his automatic pistol machine gun in hand. The clip was empty. He had nothing left. And judging by his expression, he was disappointed I was still moving.

I aimed my gun along the ground, at his head. Fired until I had nothing left, either.

His face was gone.

I couldn't get up. Despite the sun, I was cold. The pain was still there, but remote, like everything else in this dream of a reality.

At least I had the satisfaction of knowing the Wizard was dead. I'd finally killed him. Gotten rid of the only true stranger in that land between the dark and the light in which I'd been born.

Also, the satchel hadn't been hit. The monkey was safe.

I closed my eyes.

And then I was back. I had a severed head, a monkey with wings, and an audience with the Wizard.

So much for mommy thinking I was the crazy one in the family

Maybe this time it would go better.

*

It wasn't as if the Witch didn't expect a trap. Even with her fading in and out, she still managed to order a legion of Winkies to march on the Emerald City and lay siege to its walls, and had another legion patrolling the countryside and all the roads of every color.

By the time she was finally ready to go the Emerald City, herself, with Dorothy's head babbling endlessly in her lap about all the fun she was missing out on in what she called the real world, the city's citizens were more than ready to throw the gates open to her and lead her to the Wizard.

Of course, they didn't dare drag him out and throw him over the walls.

I was surprised the Wizard didn't put up a fight, shocked that the Witch listened to Dorothy talking all that time, and amazed I was allowed to remain King of the Flying Monkeys. For a monkey, that is an unusual number and range of emotions, and I must say I did not take to the air with my usual frenetic vigor when she commanded her Flying Monkeys to help her fetch the Wizard from his lair. I could sense she was not all there, though once, when she screamed for no good reason, I thought she was not all gone, either. I'd never heard the Witch scream, before.

I wanted only to help my Witch become all that she was, so I could be all that I was with her. I never thought being who and what we are would be so painful.

We broke through the five-storey doors to the Wizard's audience hall with spells and explosives. The Winkie warriors slipped and slid over the smooth, polished floor, crashing into each other and the walls as they were distracted by the Witch's screamed orders and the Wizard's flickering image demanding to know who had interrupted his meditations. It was left to the Monkeys to fly into the hall's rafters and spy the rustle of curtains in a corner. We were accustomed to dragging out hidden prey.

The Wizard, as it turned out, was a short, round man who was also tall and thin, and both had restless features. One moment he was old, the next young; he gained and lost hair in the blink of an eye; and there were even stretches of time when he was a woman.

"You attacked me," the Witch accused the Wizard, pointing at him with a long, curling finger whose tip seemed weighed down with the potency of a spell.

"I granted your damn wish," the Wizard said, with a voice that was the squeak of a rusty wheel, though he didn't have the same mouth for more than a moment. "You're back, aren't you? This is what you wanted, wasn't it?"

The Witch came closer, and she plucked a pair of eyes from the choices that were offered to her from the palette of the Wizard's shifting visage, and then a nose, a set of lips, brows, ears. She picked hair from the forest that passed beneath her palm, and traced a body in the air that the Wizard gradually settled into, until he became the man the Witch had wanted to meet, the man she'd obviously spent a lot of time imagining, a man who was most certainly not a monkey.

Her pointing finger touched his forehead and his eyes fluttered.

"Yes, thank you, this is what I wanted," she told him. "Never let it be said the Wizard didn't grant a wish." She smiled, her eyes both hungry and gentle.

My heart broke.

"That's not the way things are done," I said.

The Witch knew she'd been walking into a trap. She just didn't know who was springing it. I didn't know myself, until I saw her make the Wizard into the image she desired. I understood she'd be staying, that she had all that she wanted and dreamed of and there'd be no more strangers coming into her territory because she wouldn't be going out among them, anymore, and so they wouldn't try to reach her.

I saw the end.

Dorothy winked at me. That's right, she seemed to be saying. The Witch won't be calling for Nikko, anymore.

"What did you say?" the Witch asked, suddenly turning to me, frowning.

I flew off. What was the point of talking about

the obvious. With a screech, I marshaled my monkey kingdom and we took the place apart, stone by stone.

Monkeys are adept at all forms of destruction. Just because we cannot read an architectural plan, just because we are not engineers and cannot build an arch or lay a foundation, doesn't mean we can't pick out with unearthly precision the vulnerable points of any structure. We have the strength to fly, we certainly have the strength to move stone.

The Witch asked complicated questions at the end: "Who are you? What are you? Did I make you? If I did, how come you're not afraid of dying when I die. And if I didn't, where did you come from?"

She hurled curses at me, and spells. But the stones were already tumbling, the rafters grinding and breaking, the vaults cracking and raining down in a hail of fine wreckage and dust. She tried to keep the place together with her magic, but she was no more an engineer than the rest of us, and though her powers of creation were prodigious, having manufactured everything in this Land, including the Emerald City and the Wizard's palace, she couldn't track the fine details of our destruction any more than she could destroy the whole, mad, teeming assembly of our tribes.

We buried her in the Wizard's palace with what she'd always been afraid of, the thing she'd conquered with her final act of creation and self-destruction. We tore down the Emerald City, as well, with the help of the Winkies, though it was a loud and boisterous affair, and we piled the rubble atop the palace, just in case. Then we set fire to the mountain we'd created, and when the ash had settled, all of us who'd been her servants relieved ourselves on the pile to poison any last trace of life that might remain.

We didn't vanish. The world didn't end.

As Dorothy had said, there were lots of little parts of the Witch spread out all over, parts she'd lost or buried or tried to get rid of. More than enough to keep the place going. We survived. The hell with her.

I led my people back to the Witch's castle, freed the heads, and made the place our home. The heads advise us, and we take care of them. If they wish, we fly them around so they can see the world they've missed for so long. Some paint, using borrowed Monkey hands. Others prefer to be locked in rooms where the music they love never stops. There are even some in the Land who don't mind caressing a head resting on their laps, whispering sweet sayings into their ears, kissing their lips, allowing the bodiless heads to have their way with the parts they miss most.

The heads have become very good listeners, as well.

The Land has seen stranger love.

We are at peace. For now. I can't say how long we can hold back against the Winkies. And all the rest. The monkeys chatter, the rage builds. Flying Monkey litters fill the catacombs. Something must break loose.

There's a new queen born, I hear. A new king has been conceived. Soon, it'll be time to leave, before the children eat their old.

I'll try to wait until the last of the grudges is settled and there are no more fights brewing. I'm going to jump the rainbow and see what's on the other side. Take the veteran Flying Monkeys with me. Take up painting. Look for another Wizard. A kinder one.

A Wizard who'll grant my wish for a Witch who likes Flying Monkeys.

And isn't afraid of Wizards.

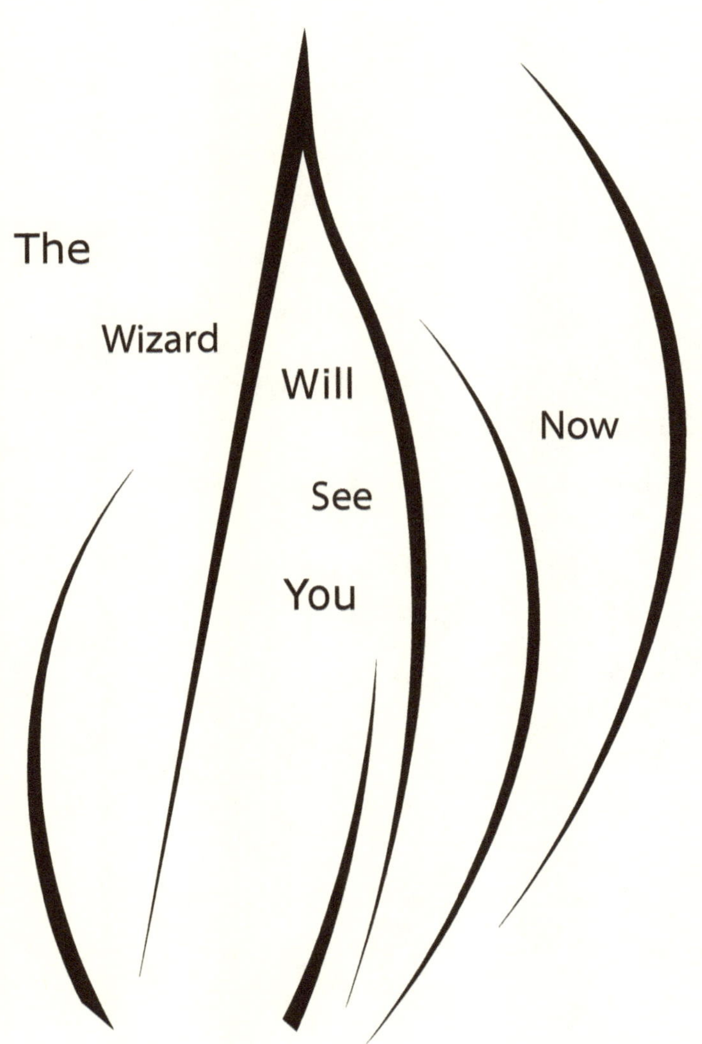
The
Wizard
Will
See
You
Now

When I was ten, my Daddy killed me.

It happened after I got sick. Threw up. In the middle of The Wizard of Oz, the musical version everyone's seen. Right at the start of the Yellow Brick Road number.

Dorothy and her band of make-believe brothers, and her little dog, too, were skipping off to Oz. The dizzies caught my head, and my stomach felt real bad, and the next thing I knew I was barfing up meat loaf and mashed potatoes all over the basement rec room floor. Good thing we had that super turf carpet stuff. Mom twitched, but saw I wasn't looking good and instead of yelling, she sent me to bed.

Dad didn't care about the mess. Didn't bother to clean it up. He just sat on the sofa, staring off, like he was set up in a stand on the edge of a meadow lining up a buck in his sights. Nothing would move him, not bird shit or kid vomit. He never checked in on me, either, once I was in bed. Mom came by a few times, took my temperature, said I had the flu and loaded me up with pills and juice. Kissed me on the cheek, and on my forehead. Held my hand.

I didn't feel so bad after I knew I wouldn't have to go to school the next day. But I didn't feel like getting up and celebrating, either. Worst thing about getting sick was missing the attack of the flying monkeys. That and the Wicked Witch of the West's Winkie guards marching into the castle.

I dreamed they were coming after me, though. Wings beating and furry hands reaching, they dove out of the clouds like a swarm of bees. I ran, beating them off, slapping their silly, wide-opened mouths shut, poking them in their big bug-eyes. The only thing that bothered me was their screeching. After a bit, the screeching nearly made sense, and I stopped to listen to what they were saying. The words didn't come together in sentences, so I listened harder, and pretty soon I recognized Mom and Dad, and that's when I woke up from my dream, hot and sweaty, but also cold.

For a few of minutes, I thought I was still in a movie. But not the Wizard of Oz.

Instead, I felt like I'd been dropped into one where the killer breaks into the house while the parents are fighting and the kids are crying and no one's paying attention to what's really going on. You know, shadows all around, silence in the corners, deep night on the other side of the windows, and the family's trapped in their own world, oblivious to who's in the house with them. Short, sharp music tells you something bad's coming.

I was in the house with them, and I was coming.

For a while, it was fun. Felt like I was stalking big game, like those cats on the Discovery Channel. Listening for the sounds of my prey. Waiting for the moment to strike. Getting ready to do a thing that was going to be fast and hard and bloody.

Then I got scared. Had a feeling something else was in the house. Watching me. Waiting. Suddenly, the movie wasn't fun. I remembered I was sick. Laying in a bed with my back to the darkness.

Maybe I was the prey. Like Dorothy, chased by the Witch.

I sat right up, heart beating like bird's. Shaking all over. Stayed frozen for a good, long while. Stared into every corner of my room, making sure no one was there. I was a little dizzy, too. And hot. Had to think hard to figure out if I was still dreaming.

The yelling got louder though it didn't sound closer. I figured Mom and Dad were fighting about me. I felt bad and got up to tell them I was sorry but I really was sick and not 'acting out' like Mom sometimes said I did because she was having my baby sister in six months. I mean, to be honest, I wasn't happy about getting a little sister. Never asked or even wished for one. Carl had a little sister and he said she kept him up at night crying and the house was crazy and they never went out anywhere anymore because of the baby. Jamal always complained about his older sister. Me, Chris and Carl thought she beat him up all the time and he was too embarrassed to tell us. We sure never messed with her. Chris had a younger one, too, but she was only a couple of years behind him and he didn't seem to mind. Sometimes when somebody's parents took us to the mall, or to a party, she'd tag along. Once she held my hand when we were going up an escalator. It was embarrassing. But kind of nice, too.

The Wizard of Oz was back in my head when I went downstairs. The monkeys were gone, but "Over the Rainbow" kept playing in my head, and I had to check to make sure I wasn't wearing ruby slippers. The guys would never let me live that one down.

And I still felt the witch, or somebody, watching me through a crystal ball.

The movie was all around me, too. The color part, only the colors were super real, while the steps I was walking on and the rail and the wall I leaned on for balance felt like cardboard fakes. It was weird feeling, like when Bobby and Jamal and Carl used to come over Saturday afternoons and we'd fast forward through every horror video we could get our hands on to watch the good parts while Mom was busy cleaning and talking on the phone and Dad was fixing something or other and they both thought we were watching the game. After the guys were gone, and Mom and Dad were sleeping, I'd be all alone in my room when those good parts ran in my head over and over, until I'd get more and more scared, because the good parts aren't so much fun when you're by yourself and it feels like it's the dark that's keeping those parts playing, over and over, in your head.

I might have been on the Yellow Brick Road, only Dorothy and her gang had left me behind and I didn't even have a dog and it was getting dark and the Wicked Witch's flying monkeys were in the clouds, getting ready to dive.

I felt like I was missing a good part, but maybe that was all right since I wasn't sure I wanted to actually be in that good part.

I was going to see the Wizard, but I didn't know why.

The yelling stopped when I reached the living room. The quiet made me more scared than when they'd been making so much noise.

I went into the kitchen.

That's where I saw Dad stabbing Mommy in the chest with a big knife.

Over and over again, like in the scary movies.

There was more blood in the kitchen than in anything I'd ever seen on TV. The sounds – Mom kind of gurgling while trying to talk and cry at the same time; the thump of Dad's fist on her chest as he smacked the knife back into her, over and over, mostly through the same hole he'd made; the squeak of sneakers on the dry part of the floor – sliced right through my head and opened me up to reality.

I wasn't in a movie.

I felt that knife go into Mommy like I was her. Cold steel kissed my heart.

The impact took my breath away.

Mommy tried raising her hand. Like she wanted to hold mine the way she used to when we crossed streets when I was little. Daddy saw me, too. But he didn't stop.

And it smelled bad: the worst parts of a Little League Port-O-Potty bathroom and the garbage can behind the meat counter at the supermarket.

I was more hurt than scared because that was Mom sliding off the kitchen table, all broken with blood coming out her mouth instead of sounds, her eyes opening wider until I was too small to notice, an invisible dust mote in her universe of pain. I wanted to call out, make her see me.

But she was looking at something else. Something behind me.

My father grunted, or maybe he growled – it

was a dog thing, anyway – and then he stopped. Stood there breathing hard like he did after he went out on a fly pattern during a weekend game of touch football with his buddies at the park.

Then Daddy said, "I'm sorry," and he walked over like he was going to pick me up and save me from whatever was coming, or whoever had done that to Mom because even though I'd seen Dad doing the stabbing what I'd seen didn't make sense. I thought I was still dreaming, and there was a killer loose in the house, but Dad was here and everything would turn out all right.

Only Dad didn't pick me up. He stuck the knife in my chest.

It wasn't as cold as I'd imagined. The steel was warm with blood.

I looked for Mommy, but she was still staring through me. I got real scared, more than any other time that night. I glanced over my shoulder because I felt something coming out of nowhere, fast and hard, reaching for me, screeching like a bat. I also didn't want to see the knife in my chest. Feeling it was bad enough.

I shook from chills and fright. My eyes burned because I was crying, but I couldn't make a sound. My chest hurt worse than when I saw Daddy stabbing Mommy.

I didn't see anything coming up from behind.

I fell down. Don't know if Daddy pushed me too hard when he put in the knife, or if I my legs gave out. Daddy watched me fall, not sad or angry or happy, just blank, like the mask the killer wears in movies when he doesn't want his face to be seen.

The kitchen tile was cold for a second, but then I didn't feel it. I stared at the ceiling, still feeling something coming, burning right through the hard floor to get to the bones of my neck.

Daddy stepped over me without bothering to see what he'd done. The knife stood tall, a pole without a flag planted in a throbbing nest of organs. I grabbed the handle with both hands. It was wood, still warm and a little wet from sweat. The knife must have been from the good set. It felt solid, a part of me, like I'd grown a horn. I pulled a little, but my chest hurt too much. And I was bleeding.

That's when I understood I was dead.

Daddy killed me. Punched through me like a roast set to be carved.

You watch enough of this stuff, you know when you're supposed to be dead.

I couldn't get up. The kitchen phone was too far to reach. There was another one on the coffee table. Low enough to get to without having to stand.

Daddy came back. Maybe he'd gone to the bathroom. Or to check out the front window. I don't know what he did, but I was crawling out on my knees and elbows, knife handle scrapping the floor, when he stepped over me again on his way into the kitchen. His face was still blank, like a blackboard full of answers the teacher had erased just before giving a pop quiz.

I kept going, though I was tired, and it was hard to breathe. I didn't look back. I could hear him grunting in there, though, doing that dog-thing again. There was a wet, pounding sound, too

Maybe Daddy found another knife. Maybe he'd found something else to kill.

I reached the phone, called 911. Told the operator I was dead, and that Daddy killed me and Mommy. Then I hung up because there was nothing else to say. The operator called back and asked me questions. It got harder to answer, but she told me to stay with her, and that I was a good little boy and brave, and help was coming and she didn't want me to leave. So I stayed. Talking to her, I forgot all about whatever was chasing me.

Then the police came. Broke down the front door. Walked right in. An officer stood over me with his gun drawn. He stared at the knife and went pale. I was surprised there wasn't much noise coming from the kitchen. I figured the police would be upset, and so would my Dad, and they get into an argument. But everything was quiet.

Then the police mumbled and their radios squawked back, talking about how Daddy killed himself with a knife. I hoped whatever had been after me had settled for him, instead. After that, things got blurry.

I wound up in the hospital. Once I woke up, floating through halls looking up at ceiling lights and faces, some masked. I didn't like breathing because I could smell liquorice and peppermint and disinfectant.

I thought for a while that I was on the way to heaven, or maybe hell. Then I figured whatever Mommy had seen coming had finally caught up and as dragging me to its secret lair.

But all the scared had bled out of me, by then, so I didn't care. Besides, I was already dead. What else could happen?

I woke up again in a nice quiet room, but couldn't stay awake for long. Nurses and doctors came to visit. They looked real happy to see me. That made me feel good. Like I was alive.

I stayed in the hospital until I thought that's where I was supposed to go after I died, but the doctors told me no, I was alive, and all I had to was keep getting better and I'd live a long life.

It wasn't bad in there, though some of the other kids I was with didn't last very long. Sometimes the adults cried because they were happy someone was going home, and sometimes they cried because someone died. I never cried. But I made sure I looked sad when everyone else was, and cheer with the rest when somebody left.

My stalker was gone. Maybe it lost my trail in the hospital, or forgot about me because it thought I was dead. Every now and then, I felt it might be waiting outside. I looked out the window a lot, but never saw anything lurking in the streets, on the rooftops, or in the clouds. I stared into mirrors, looking over my shoulder, but nothing ever showed up.

I wasn't sure I was actually alive. But at least I wasn't completely dead, either. My burning chest was a reminder.

People were very nice. If I smiled, and talked a little, and gave out compliments on how good people were to me and how much I appreciated what they were doing, people went even more out of their way to be kind. The scar helped, too.

I tried telling Carl, Bobby and Jamal when they

came to visit that all you have to do is make people like you and they'll be so nice, but they didn't believe me. They were fidgety, like I was a new kid in school and a little too weird. I guess I can't blame them because I'd never wanted to visit anyone in a hospital, much less someone dead, or who'd come back from the dead. That was too much like a horror movie.

The foster home they eventually sent me to wasn't as bad as the other kids at the hospital said it would be. I was careful, did what I was supposed to, found people to protect me by being nice to them. I learned that fast enough. You had to be a little innocent, like you didn't really know everything you did know, but you also had to show you weren't stupid. When I got the hang of the rules of the game, more good things happened than bad ones.

Not that the good things that happened after I died changed anything.

My daddy still killed me.

Sure, I survived. Or came back, like they do in movies. Or I got another life, like in a video game. But getting killed in real life is nothing like any game. And watching somebody getting killed for real is different, too.

I never stopped watching horror movies, though they didn't scare me, anymore. Even got into playing video games, when the good ones came out that made everything happening almost seem real. Still play when I need to get away. But I always know where they get things wrong, where they could never ever get things right like I've seen they are.

I never watched the Wizard of Oz, again. And

nothing I couldn't see ever chased me. Not until I got the idea to look for the Wizard.

I just grew up. Went to a different town, a new school. Got to know another family. Called other people Mom and Dad. Had a brother and a couple of sisters. All of them a lot like me: none of us came from our new Mom and Dad. All of us were orphans.

That's kind of an ugly word. Don't like it much, even now. Got into trouble about it at school. Had some fights. Learned you couldn't be nice all the time.

Fire, accident, and a runaway dad after the mother died of cancer, were the things that happened to make the other orphans in my foster family.

Even if the kids had actually been caught in the fire and the accident, even if they'd died and come back, like me, they still couldn't know what it was like to be killed. All the bad things that happened to them were accidents. They might have watched their parents die, or woken up one day to find them gone, but they hadn't felt the things I had. They'd never felt anything coming after them.

Sometimes I still miss Carl, Jamal and Bobby.

Growing up, I missed things because I'd been dead. Mommy, for one, though I forgot soon enough exactly what she looked like. Even in the pictures I kept, she didn't seem right. Still doesn't. I know that's me, Mommy and Daddy in them, but I feel like we're all impersonators. Special effects. Stunt doubles. Pod people from that movie they keep re-making.

Mommy used to dance around and sing to "I Want Candy" by Siouxie and the Banshees, and I used to pretend I was one of the band members from the music video, but now I can't even recognize the song when I download it off the internet, or the band when I see the video on cable flashback shows.

I miss the jelly pizzas Mommy used to make for lunch from leftover breakfast pancakes. I make them from the same mix and jelly, and I heat them up in the oven, not the microwave, just like she did, but they still taste like sick-sweet cardboard. And though another mother kissed me goodnight for a lot of years after she was gone, it was never the same. Those kisses always felt like a fly landing on my cheek or forehead, something I wanted to brush away because it was dirty and annoying.

I miss Daddy. Even though he killed me, he wasn't all bad. He took me to baseball games, movies, and out hunting and fishing, and let me watch when he played touch football with his friends. We had a good time together. Sometimes he slept through movies or didn't pay attention to a game. His friends yelled at him for dropping a ball. Maybe he had something on his mind. Or he was just doing all these things to kill time, and he was bored.

I wish he'd kept on killing time.

I wish I'd had a choice on what I could miss, like school, and homework, and bullies. The ache in the place where I got stabbed. And getting killed.

I would have been fine missing out on the Wizard, too.

It's the movie that gave me the idea to look for him.

The movie of the Wizard of Oz stayed with me all the time I was growing up, a ghost image that'd been burned into my brain that night. I remembered my favorites, the flying monkeys and the witch's guards, but they weren't as important as the Wizard. The one in charge, the one everyone had to see. The one I'd been on my own private, fever-induced Yellow Brick Road to see that night. No matter what I did or who I was with, there was always a part of me stuck in the Land of Oz, on the Yellow Brick Road, off the see the Wizard but all alone, with the monkeys and the marching guards coming after me. And something else.

I didn't need to see the damned thing, anymore. I was living the movie, stuck in Oz, looking for the way to go back home.

When I was nearly done with high school, close to graduation and having to make up my mind about what I was going to do with the rest of my life, feeling like I was dying all over again so much I felt that knife in my chest just like it had been when Daddy put it there, cold and hard, I said in a bar that I needed to find the Wizard so I could get a brain, a heart, and some courage to find the way home. It was just something stupid to say when people kept asking what I was doing after school.

I laughed hard about that one, and though everyone was as drunk as I was, they didn't laugh so hard because they didn't get it, and the bouncer threw me out because I'd stopped being funny and suddenly he remembered I was still a minor.

Sitting out there on the sidewalk by myself, head spinning, dizzy, sore and sick, like I felt that night, all the broken pieces of what I'd been carrying for years came together.

I understood what I had to do. Why I'd been killed and why I'd come back.

I really <u>was</u> supposed to see the Wizard. Just like Dorothy.

That was him, that day. Great and powerful. Hiding behind his curtain. Puffed up with blood and pain and all that stabbing. Making things happen, and watching.

Stalking.

Mommy saw him. If I thought about it long enough, if I remembered every last detail, I was sure I could see her eye's reflection of what she'd been looking at, the thing she'd seen when I'd been lost to her.

A mirage of a man. The sliver of a shadow. That's who I'd felt, right behind me, through the fever dream of the movie I'd fallen into.

The Wizard, granting a terrible wish for my Mom. Sending her home. Like he did Dad.

The Wizard let everything make sense. He was the missing ingredient, the thing I didn't see but knew was there. The one who could explain why my Mom and Dad had to go and why I couldn't go with them. He could tell me where I really belonged – with the living, or the dead, or someplace else – and send me there. He could tell me what should come next.

But why hadn't he explained what I was supposed to be and do when he came for Mom and Dad?

Something wrong. With him. Me. Us.

I'd been scared. He was scarey. Maybe I should have stayed. Waited for him to catch me. But I'd looked for what was hunting me. I'd tried to spot him. And I'd been right there, in the blood. No place to hide, no way to escape. He could have taken me if he wanted to. I couldn't have stopped him. Neither could my parents.

He must have had plans for me. Or maybe he was scared, too.

Of me.

Like the Wicked Witch always seemed scared of Dorothy. She didn't go after Dorothy herself, she sent the flying monkeys. Because, after all, Dorothy did kill her sister. And the little girl could make friends, and had lots of them. Turned out, she had good reason to be scared.

I wasn't sure about the Wizard being scared of me. But I did feel I had something special that kept him from ever catching up. Nothing obvious, like ruby red slippers. But a reason why the Wizard wouldn't take me like he took Mom and Dad. Why he just watched. Why I didn't stay dead.

Being dead must have been part of the plan. Something special had to happen to anybody coming back from the dead. You lose a life, but you gain a secret.

Maybe the Wizard gave me a power because he felt sorry I wasn't going where my Mom and Dad went. Maybe what I went through was like radiation, from getting too close too an atom bomb blast, or the Wizard, that changes you into a mutant superhero or supervillain.

But what I didn't get right away was, what was the power?

Could I survive more stabbings? I didn't exactly want to try finding out if that was true.

Was I going to go crazy like my Dad and kill

everything I was supposed to love? That might be a hard one to test, since I never really loved my orphan brothers and sisters, or my adoptive parents. That little sister Mommy had been carrying never got born, so I didn't get a chance with her. And even though I wasn't a virgin by any stretch of the imagination, that didn't mean I'd fallen in love with anyone I'd banged. Even the pregnant ones.

And then it hit me. I was the only one who knew there *was* a Wizard.

I'd felt him that night, even before I saw what was happening in the kitchen. Before the knife.

I asked around. People thought I was crazy. The Wizard is a character in a book, they said. Or in a movie, if they didn't know about the books. The few people who thought they knew there was a Wizard gave me stupid answers, like it was an electronics store, or the name of a team, or a game. They said the Wizard was a computer program, virus, or hacker. Some even said it was the name of a drug, and they could get me some if I'd just wait fifteen minutes.

Nobody ever talked about the Wizard the way I knew him: someone who makes a daddy kill his son and his son's mommy. Only I had the power of knowing there was a Wizard, and what he was capable of doing.

But trying to describe who and what I knew the Wizard to be made me sound as crazy as people thought I was for even asking about him. All the power did was set me apart; it didn't actually help me do anything. It was like being a reject from the Legion of Substitute Super-Heroes.

So I was stuck for a while. I understood I had to

find the Wizard so I could figure out what I was supposed to be, and the power of knowledge was supposed to help me. But how?

On top of that, I was worrying about how to even ask for what I wanted when I did find him. The Wizard wasn't exactly helpful in the movie. He put Dorothy through tests, and he lied, played tricks, and in the end actually left her behind.

In reality, he was a mystery, which didn't help me forget what I'd felt when he was close by, just out of sight, a secret presence presiding over the dying flesh of my parents.

How was I supposed to ask if he abandoned me as a mercy, or a punishment? What if the thing I was supposed to do for him was a secret even I couldn't be trusted with? Maybe I'd find him pissed off, because I hadn't done what he wanted me to when he left me to live. Or, if the time hadn't come yet for me to fulfill his purpose, he'd be pissed for wasting my time, and his, tracking him down and asking him stupid questions.

Or, he might be in one of his moods and not want to be bothered answering questions and granting wishes. He could lose his patience with me, and do what Daddy did. Do it right, this time.

Take me in a way that would hurt worse than the way Mom and Dad went.

That's when I wondered about how badly I wanted to meet this Wizard, and if I really needed to go home, again.

But the Wizard was the big knot in my life, tying everything together so I couldn't move forward or backward. I had to see him, no matter what the consequences. Even if I turned out like my father. Even if it was going to hurt.

But there were so many questions to get through before I could ask the ones that really mattered. How was I going to find the Wizard? Where was that Yellow Brick Road leading to Oz? What could get me through the gates of Oz to the Wizard?

I tried not to think about what the Wizard felt like, coming up behind me, reaching out of the blindness of my darkest places.

I read *The Wonderful Wizard Oz*, and then the *Marvelous* one, which I didn't like because Dorothy wasn't in it, and the third one, when she was, but she met the Nome King, and then I gave up because I didn't want to get distracted with too many characters. I found other versions of the movie, and comics, and all kinds of things people collected. But I couldn't catch a clue.

I dabbled in magic, since the books and movie were full of the stuff. Didn't believe in it. The knife had me pinned firmly to reality, and none of the fever movie dreams from that day could shake me loose. But the Wizard drove me to try. I consulted witches and seers, attended séances, made pilgrimages to Salem, New Orleans, and everywhere magical in between. Even Orlando.

I got to thinking about Mom, Dad, and the Wizard, and how they'd found a way to the Wizard. Funny, until then, I'd thought what had happened had simply been something crazy, random, without explanation. Never figured my mother, or father, or maybe even both, made things happen the way they did. Never thought they'd wanted the same thing I did.

Sometimes, kids can be so stupid.

I went back to the old neighborhood, hung out in the bars and churches looking for hints of any cults back then, and if my parents had been involved. All I found was that the cops asked the same thing.

After a bit, the psycho supernatural stuff started getting to me. That, and remembering how my Mom and Dad were, how everything seemed normal, until the end. I remembered Daddy's eyes. And Mommy's. At the very end.

Maybe Dad, or Mom, or the both of them, really had made things play out the way they did, to see the Wizard. They'd obviously had their own questions, their own needs, and having me or each other sure hadn't satisfied them. Maybe they constructed their own Yellow Brick Road.

So I started making up ceremonies and celebrations. Offerings. Sacrifices. Even if I still didn't believe in any of it. After all, I'd said my prayers at dinner, bedtime, church, with my real parents, and the adoptive ones. People believed in the angels and devils, miracles, their own versions of the Wizard. There were all kinds of religious rites. It seemed like people had been calling to their versions of the Wizard for a long time. Why not invent my own system?

It seemed to work for Mom and Dad.

I went with the old school. Aztec style. Right out of the History Channel. Blood and flesh.

Just like Daddy.

I picked up a big carving knife like the one Dad used on me and Mom, intent on carving up some flesh, or at least chopping off some fingers. When I had the thing in my hand, all I could do was slice open a little cut and drain some blood. Even for that, I was shaking all over. My scar turned cold. The handle was slippery with my sweat, like it had been with Mommy's blood. The cut was mostly an accident.

I'd written a kind of prayer to go along with the ceremony, cribbing lines from the movie, ending with a chant of, "there's no place like home." Seemed silly even when I wrote it, and ridiculous with the knife in my hand.

Even worse, bleeding didn't make the Wizard appear. No Yellow Brick Road.

Sacrificing someone else was another possibility, but for it to work, I thought it had to be someone close, like what Dad did with me and Mom. I didn't have anyone to offer. And besides, I'd have to be ready, like Dad had been, to actually kill someone

Honestly, I just didn't think I could do it.

I threw the knife away. Magic wasn't working for me.

I was out of ideas. My brain was ragged running circles around the Wizard, him being a secret I knew, a destination I had to reach. But there was no end to the circle. I was stuck in a movie loop, chanting "there's no place like home" and "somewhere over the rainbow" over and over. Lost in the woods, on my own, with lions, and tigers, and bears, oh my, and the only way out going straight through the Wizard. Just like Dorothy.

Only there wasn't a Yellow Brick Road. No munchkins, or Good Witches, no merry band of straw or tin men, or even a cowardly lion to point me in the right direction.

I drifted. Left my adoptive parents' town, skipped college, went out on my own looking for the Yellow Brick Road in the real world.

Worked jobs no one else would touch. Did things people shouldn't. Found out being bad to people often got you more than being nice.

But no matter how bad I was, or good, the Wizard never appeared.

Found the fields of poppy, instead, where you forget.

Got into sticking a needle in my arm. Followed another color of road, heading for a different kind of home.

I still brought up the Wizard, when I remembered, like I was on automatic pilot, with the people I dealt with on the street: junkies, homeless, crazies. Some picked up on what I said. Quite a few claimed to have been in Oz, to know the Wizard, to even be the Wizard. Or to know where I could find him, if I helped them out a little.

They didn't know. Big surprise.

Even through the smack, I never stopped needing that Yellow Brick Road.

It was from watching myself shoot up that I figured out where Road started.

Needle sticking got to be like Dad stabbing Mom. Every time I shot up, I thought about that night. Felt the knife go into me, the Wizard at my back. I thought about the blood, and how Mom and Dad were supposed to love each other, and me; how much Dad, or Mom, or both of them had given up to see the Wizard.

What could they have wanted from the Wizard

that they didn't already have?

I wasn't ready for an answer. I don't think you can ever be.

But that question didn't matter. Couldn't.

I was shaking. Rattling. The wind was picking up all my thoughts and scattering them across the fields. The sky was dark. A twister was coming, coming for to carry me away. Let it come. Let it come.

Hell. I'd been riding that twister all my life. It was always here.

Forget about Mom and Dad wanting to see the Wizard. Forget about love and sacrifice and wanting things at too terrible a cost. And forget about magic. That wasn't real.

Arms pitted with needle marks was real.

Holes. They weren't much different than the one Daddy made in my chest.

Wounds.

That's where the Road started. The hole in my chest.

The whirlwind swept me higher, carried me farther. I spun and sailed and fell until I couldn't fall no more, and where I crashed was the place where my life left me. That's where the Yellow Brick Road started. The place where the knife stuck out of my chest, where I died.

But the hole was half the Road. The other half was missing. The knife Daddy used to kill me. That was the rest of the long, winding Yellow Brick Road that would take me all the way to Oz and the Wizard.

Everything seemed so much clearer once I understood what I had to do.

I went into rehab. It wasn't so hard, as long as I kept in mind what I needed more than the poppy fields.

Went back to the cops who'd busted me on the street, showed them I'd straightened out. Steered them to a few bad guys. Enough to get them interested in a major bust. I worked with them, getting in deep on both sides, close enough to get myself killed if I wasn't careful.

But being dead taught me how to get people to like me.

Tell them what they want to hear, give them what they want. Seduce them with fantasy, even challenge them with reality, but never let them know you're in control. Be friendly. Look vulnerable. Keep your distance. Stay safe.

The cops warned me about feeling nervous because of the danger. But none of the people they were after were the Wizard. None of them made me want to look over my shoulder at what might be coming. They were amateurs.

The busts were major. I did my duty. Testified. I was a good witness. The jury liked me and wouldn't buy the defense tactics that tore down my character and attacked my motives for working with the police.

They had no idea.

The police appreciated the turn I'd taken. Got to know my story. After the trial, they saw me get a job driving a bus, settle into a real apartment, become a citizen again. No more street life. As if that would have been an option.

I never told them about the visit from a friend of the people I'd helped send to jail. Didn't want to spoil the nice rep I'd worked so hard to earn.

I moved way across town, not wanting any more visits, but kept in touch with the cops I knew. Dropped by, occasionally. Congratulated them on the promotions they'd earned because of the risks I'd taken. Kept the reputation I'd earned alive and well.

I never asked the detectives for anything. They were too smart to trust me that much, or get involved with what I was really after. But you'd be surprised what goes on in the back offices of a precinct house, and how far a good reputation and a sympathetic ear can get you with officers sentenced to desk duty, and with secretaries and clerks who never see any action, but think they're good judges of character, and are maybe eager to do a few good deeds themselves, even if the deed in question is a little bizarre.

I learned that nobody, at least nobody sane, says they're looking for the Wizard. But you'd be surprised how many are, in their own little ways.

It took quite a few years, but one day I found the right person, who felt just sorry enough for me while admiring me at the same time, who thought they understood why I needed to have what had been locked up in a warehouse for longer than they'd been working in the department, and who was just resentful enough at being cast in a civil service netherworld to lash out in a safe, reasonable, and perfectly understandable act of rebellion.

It was like I was their Wizard. I gave them everything they needed to make them feel good, like they'd gone home to a place they'd always wanted but never knew existed.

They were more like my munchkins, putting me on the road I'd been looking for.

I got the knife back that my Daddy used to kill Mommy and me.

My Yellow Brick Road.

It was kind of funny, holding it in my hands again. Free this time, not stuck in my chest. I put the point up against my skin, on the faint outline of the scar where it went in the first time. I felt like it wanted to go back in, nestle back into bone and muscle. I was cold all over.

What came next wasn't easy.

Once you find the road, you have to learn to walk it. But I didn't know how. I thought knowing what to do would be simple, obvious, like putting one foot in front of the other. I wouldn't even have to skip and dance, like Dorothy.

But with the knife in my hand and the point resting on bare skin, suddenly things didn't seem so obvious. Was I supposed to stab myself in the chest? That didn't seem reasonable. I'd been down that road, though a part of me wanted to try again. And doing what Dad had done was still out of the question. I wasn't really that nice, but I wasn't that bad, either.

So I stuck the blade point first into the butcher block cutting board on my kitchen counter and let it stand there like a monument. Or a road marker. Or a statue of an ancient and bloody god.

And everyday I came home to that knife, and sometimes I'd cut tomatoes and cucumbers with it, and other days I'd sprinkle wine or flour or spices, whatever I had on hand, over the steel as an offering to the Road and the Wizard. Sometimes I'd slice open a little cut on my finger and let some blood pour out. It was still a damn good knife.

I didn't expect anything to happen, and nothing did.

But the ritual made me feel connected to what I'd been hunting for so long. I knew the Wizard was out there. I had a feeling, after looking for him so long, that he knew I was out here, too.

I stared at the knife every night after I came home from my bus route, going around in circles all day taking people back and forth on their safe little journeys during their ordinary days. I imagined the steel in my mother. In me. I remembered the look on my father's face, and how Mommy watched something behind me come closer. There were days when the hair at the back of my neck would stand and I'd get a chill.

The knife was a good one, like I said. Bright and silver. Shiny. I could see my reflection on the broad side of its blade. If I came close up, I had a view of one of my eyes I could fall into.

What's the eye, if not a pit.

I rooted around deep in the reflection, searching for the Road. My head ached, and the old hole in my chest hurt, but I stayed with the pain, didn't shoot up, hit the bottle, or run away. Just lived with what that knife had done to me, like I was sure I was supposed to, like the Wizard wanted me to, and I didn't try to get away. I got closer, went deeper, crying, shaking. I rolled up into a ball on the cold kitchen floor, throwing up like I'd done that night, sick and full of fever.   I n my eye's reflection, blood flowed from the old wound, ran along the knife's edge, to the handle and my father's fingers. Fresh blood mingled with my mother's, still staining the steel, and I surged like a storm tide through Mommy and Daddy and all that they had been, great big monsters going crazy like out of a Godzilla movie, and to what they were now, buried under the earth, dust.

And I woke up on the Road, knowing where I had to go: to my parents' graves. A place I'd never been to or would have thought to go.

I was off to see the Wizard, at last. Back at the old killing ground.

They were buried in different cemeteries, of course. I visited them during the day. My aunt still kept up Mom's plot.

She lived far away but had come to the hospital once to tell me stories about the two of them growing up, the trouble they made and got into, the games they played, the boys they liked, and how Mom was always hungry for the new and the different which always made her reach a little farther than anyone else dared for the things she wanted. I didn't know about any of the things she was talking about back then. I guess she was trying to explain my own mother to me, to ease the pain. But Mom was Mommy. At least until she was dead.

My aunt also came to the foster home a couple of times, but never offered to take me away. She always sent Christmas money. We lost touch after I took off. It was nice to see she still cared about family.

My father's grave didn't have a stone. It was in a wild, hilly part of the cemetery where there weren't many plots. But I found his little marker, with its anonymous identifying numbers and letters.

Didn't bother clearing away the empty beer cans and fast food container. Even took a piss on the patch of dirt. It's not like anyone was around. Afterwards, I ached for the parts I missed about him more than ever.

I paid another visit at night. Hopped the fence at Mom's place first. No kids around, which meant there was probably a night watchman, so I was careful. Moved slow, stayed on the path I'd memorized using the big crypts and statuary as markers, didn't make noise. There was enough moonlight.

After I stuck the knife in the earth over her coffin, I lay down flat on the ground and stared at the broad, shiny blade, into the reflection of my eye, by the light of a small flashlight I kept hooded with a free hand, the smell of green growth and brown rot rich and ripe in my lungs.

I never looked away, even when I was shaking, eyes stinging, tears running down my cheeks. I never checked out what was rustling in the brush; didn't run away when something ran across my back, light but solid, with little claws that ripped through my shirt and scratched my skin; didn't turn when I thought I heard a girl's voice call my name, softly, like the breeze ruffling pine, willow and oak.

But I wanted to call out: Mommy?

Instead, I fell into the black heart of my own eye, into the hole in my chest, my mother's grave, as if the twister that had picked me up and carried me for so long had started up again, throwing me deeper into the Land of Oz.

I looked out at the world through my mother's death haze, at her past. Childhood memories, and the stupid little things my aunt had told me about her, popped back into my head like lightning bugs. A few quick, sudden flashes, and I finally caught a bigger picture of a wild-child heart trapped in strict upbringing and a traditional family: my mother, not Mommy, as a rough sketch of an unhappy woman far from complete.

And in the incomplete puzzle of her life, I saw the hole in her, the one that was there before Dad carved another one her. It felt as if our secret, empty hearts called out to each other across time and death. I was closer to her in that moment that I'd been to anyone, ever, and I remembered what love was supposed to feel like.

She really had been looking for the Wizard, just like me. Stumbling along on her own Yellow Brick Road. And the road had taken her to the kitchen, with my Dad, where she'd found the Wizard. Seen him, right behind me.

From what I remember, I think she wished she hadn't.   I still didn't know what she'd been trying to ask for when she lay dying and croaking on the table where I found her. I was grateful for that.

A final piece of her settled in me like a dove in a nest. I shut my eyes, breaking the connection before I fell too deep, so far I'd never get away. I turned the flashlight off and rolled on to my back, breathing hard, sweating and exhausted like I'd run a marathon.

But I was still racing, not through a park or a city landscape, but in my mind, through canyons of memory. I wasn't running for a prize, but to escape my father coming after me, neither angry nor happy, knife in hand.

Ahead of me, at the finish line, someone dashed out from the side, arms open to greet and hold me. Not my mother. Or my father.

I opened my eyes, shaking, a cry choking my throat, desperate for and terrified of an embrace.

The little girl, naked and floating a foot off of the ground above and behind me, glowed like a full moon. But unlike the moon, her light didn't brighten the surroundings. I could see through to the tree trunks behind her.

"Who are you?" I asked, then broke into a fit of coughing.

She stared with flat eyes from a smooth, oval face whose only accent was the sad curve of her lips, like a stuffed and mounted animal. Black hair hung limp to her frail shoulders. She was flat-chested, nearly skeletal, but the bones beneath her tightly-drawn skin didn't quite seem to all be in the right places. Her silence made me think maybe Mommy really had been calling me, before.

I never believed in magic. Not in the supernatural, either. The Wizard was something else. He took up a lot of room. After him, there wasn't space to believe in anything more. So even though I was in a cemetery in the middle of the night performing an odd ritual with disturbing, even frightening results, I never thought I'd run into an actual spirit.

I got up, pulled the knife out of the ground. She stared at it, and her face changed, eyes getting wider, lips parting, smooth brow suddenly dark, like something else was breaking through the little girl shell. The knife felt cold in my hand.

For a moment I thought I'd come up on the Wizard without knowing it. Or the Wizard had found to me. Someone had switched the reels in the projection booth and I was in another movie. An old one, from my childhood, in which I was being watched. All kinds of thoughts bumped into each other in my head, and I tried to pin point the question I wanted answered, the thing I needed to get, the wish the Wizard had to fulfill.

I put the knife in the bag I'd carried it in, and the little girl went back to being a small, smooth shell. More than fright stirred and shifted inside me.

I still had my mother's eye in me, a fading sunset of another life, and through her vision I felt a bond with the girl that I didn't understand. Then a trickle of resentment startled me, even as it grew into a gushing stream of hot and bitter bile that made me want to take the knife back out.

Of course. She was my sister. Unborn. Not whole. So much missing from her she wouldn't even know what to ask for if she ever did meet the wizard.

There was no point asking for her name. She'd done well just by growing up as much as she had, however badly she'd done it, probably by modeling herself on the well-dressed and sad children who'd come to the cemetery over the years for funerals and to put flowers on the graves of their parents. Maybe the need to grow was the only thing she'd brought out from her mother's womb, the only thing that kept her anchored to the living world. Or perhaps the Wizard's touch had sparked her spirit to life before its time. Whatever her origin, my sister had long ago reached the limit of her development and remained a nameless little girl I might have grown to love, long ago. "Who do you want to be?" I asked. "The scarecrow, tin man, or lion?"

She didn't answer, and I turned away and left. There was nothing I could give her. It wasn't until I was over the fence that I noticed she was following me. If the night watchman saw her glowing form skimming the tops of grave stones, he didn't say anything to stop us from leaving.

I drove off, heading for my father's burial ground, more scared of what I'd see through his eyes than my baby sister who really wasn't. I left her behind quick enough, but somewhere on the interstate she found me and re-appeared sitting cross-legged on the back seat. She didn't look out the front or side windows into the darkness, or at the lit-up signs and storefronts, or the houses. She stared at me, at what she could catch of me in the rear view mirror: my eyes.

She was pulling the same trick I'd picked up with the knife. Diving into the past through grave pit eyes to catch what she'd missed, to search for the path she was supposed to follow.

I was sorry that she thought I was the one to lead her to someplace that would fill her emptiness.

The cemetery where my father was buried was a little more active. Girls giggled and bottles clinked from shadows near the entrance, where I entered through a hole in the fence. Deeper in, heavy metal music pulsed and droned faintly from inside a crypt. A dog barked at me, or maybe at my could-have-been sister, from atop another crypt with broken windows and doors fallen off their hinges. No one stopped me, or ran away from the glowing little girl a half-dozen steps at my back. I didn't bother being careful with the flashlight beam.

My father's grave was quiet. I stuck the knife in the bare, unhallowed dirt. My sister bristled. A storm was building in and through her, picking up strands of dark hair, whipping shadows across the brightness of her face. Her gaze was fixed on the knife.

I went down on my belly, peered into my eye's reflection. The wild things that had toyed with me at my mother's grave never came close in this place.

I felt the knife punch through me, cold and hard, as if my father had returned from the dead and used it again.

If I could come back, why couldn't he?

But why would he? He'd gone over the rainbow and wasn't turning around. He'd kept going straight on the same Yellow Brick Road he'd followed stabbing into me. That was my road, the one I wanted to get on. So I did.

And fell again, suddenly, as if the ground had been pulled away and I was plunging through a crack in the surface of things, slipping away from the reality I understood and losing myself in the places beneath, and beyond, what appeared to be true.

My sister lay beside me, though the blade would not hold her image or even her glow. She hissed in my ear, perhaps in warning, or hatred.

So maybe she could speak, if she had something to say.

The Road turned on a hairpin, and my old wound twisted, scar tissue writhing to life, healed bone and muscle and skin breaking, tearing, shredding, for Daddy. I bled, and I shivered. I made a sound half way between a grunt and growl. Like a dog.

The eye that looked back at me was no longer my own, or my mother's. It was Dad's.

I looked back at myself through a reflected eye, seeing the man I'd become: straight black hair, long nose, thin lips. A delicate face, frail, like Mommy, especially at the end.

The eyes were my father's. Everybody used to say that when I was little.

Through his eyes, I saw the hole my father had made in my chest. And then I saw deeper and farther and more clearly, the rarified crystalline air of all the things I did not miss about him magnifying the emptiness at the heart of the mystery of my murdering father.

He was digging.

And then I realized that he hadn't made that hole in me, only cleared away the clutter that had kept it hidden. Exposed what had always been in me. That's all he'd been doing with Mommy, too. Clearing away the detritus of life. We'd always been mortally wounded. He'd just wanted to get at the reality of who and what we were.

That hole, that wound, was not just the place where the Yellow Brick Road began. It's where it also ended: the hollow of our deepest pain, the burrow under our flesh where something we needed was missing.

The empty nest of our lost dream: the Wizard's palace.

And through my Daddy's eyes, I saw he hadn't been trying to kill us, or even teach us the truth about what we all carry as part of our burden of living. He hadn't been crazy. He'd found his Yellow Brick Road, tumbled into the pit of his own pain, all on his own.

He'd seen the Wizard.

Wished his wish.

And the price the Wizard had asked for the thing Daddy needed, the impossible task the Wizard had set on him to perform, was nothing like slaying a wicked witch and bringing back her broom. This was the real world, not a simple movie. The cost had been to raise the tempest that would bring us, sooner or later, to the Land of Oz and the Yellow Brick Road, and to clear the way so that Mommy and I could find and follow the road to the Wizard's palace on our own.

The Wizard knew all about sacrifice.

Mommy's journey had been a short one, once Daddy set her straight. Mine should have been quick, too.

I never found the name of the emptiness that drove my father to find the Wizard. There'd been no brother or sister from his side of the family to tell me stories and secrets of his growing up, which might have brought him into sharper focus. Only his pain made him crisp and clear for me when I looked into the blade for him.

I don't know what the Wizard gave him for his sacrifice. I have no idea if it was all worth it. I'm happy not knowing.

I do know that I fell asleep on my father's grave that night, and when I woke I was alone with a failing flashlight casting its flickering beam on the knife that had killed me. My sister was gone, if she'd ever been there. I wasn't even sure I could see any reflection in the blade's dull steel.

Maybe it had all been a dream.

I pulled the knife out of the ground and put it away, feeling stupid. I'd wasted a lot of time and energy so far, and what did I have to show for it? Visits to my parents' graves. A knife that might have been involved in a homicide, attempted homicide, and a suicide; or maybe an evidence clerk's practical joke.

I should have gone to college. Maybe tracked down my old friends and started watching movies on the couch with them, again. Slept in fields of poppy, instead of spending so much time searching for a figment of a terrified childhood imagination.

I went back through the graveyard, stumbling through darkness. I passed a couple making love on an abandoned grave with a broken and weathered head stone half-hidden by bushes. They never saw me, didn't hear my footsteps. Even ignored my sister's reappearance.   She'd come back, like a moth drawn to light. Or maybe she hadn't wanted to wait for me by Daddy's grave. Her glow as she floated over the lovers failed to illuminate their bodies, and they remained humping shadows in the night.

I stopped. My sister looked to me. Whatever storm that had raged inside her seemed to have spent itself. She was round-faced and calm, again, a naked little girl looking for a home. I held my hand out, expecting her to take it like any kid's supposed to with an older brother. But she didn't.

Maybe she hadn't seen anyone hold hands in all those years she spent growing up in the cemetery.

I left her descending on to the couple, fading as she merged with desperate, living flesh that housed a mother's womb and a father's seed. I hoped I'd been her wizard, or at the very least her munchkin, and brought her the life she'd been hanging around waiting to have.

I went home. Back to work.

Found a wife, had a couple of kids. Tried to forget the Yellow Brick Road in new fields of poppy. Watched a lot of sports and drank a lot of beer.

But I can never forgot. Every now and then, I catch a glimpse of the flying monkeys overhead. I hear the guards chanting as they march.

I know the Wizard waits inside me to grant whatever I desire. For a price.

After all I've gone through, there's no escape. I'm stuck in Oz, a servant in the Wizard's palace. I stand at the gate and ask, who goes there, when others come knocking. I ask for secret passwords and deny easy access. I hustle those few visitors who make it through the gate into the palace, and bring them into the antechamber of the Wizard's Hall. Here we sit, the junkies, the homeless and the crazies, petitioners and guards and gatekeepers, doing our duty, waiting our turn.

I try to make certain my wife and kids aren't searching too hard for the Yellow Brick Road.

But we all come down the Road, whether we know it or not, searching for deliverance, for hope, for whichever of the many things we do not, cannot, and never will have, in the company of those we hope we love, or all alone. We weather the witches and the flying monkeys, the tricks and the impossible traps, and some of us even fight through the sweet poppy fields of pleasure and the comfort of forgetfulness, all for an audience with the reluctant Wizard who we think will grant our wish.

Daddy went to the Wizard. Made his wish. And the Wizard did what all wizards do – named his price.

Daddy said yes. Got a knife. Killed me.

I haven't figured out my wish. What do I want? A brain? A heart? Forgetfulness? To go home? Never to have been dead? So many choices.

Maybe one of them is love.

But I have the knife. And a question: who's the little man standing behind the curtain in the great Wizard's Hall?

I think I know why the Wizard didn't take me when I was young. Wizards get tired. Sometimes, they want to go home, too. Like in the movies.

We don't always have to know what we want before we ask for it. I think the Wizard senses when you're ready. He keeps watching, in his little crystal ball, and lets you come to him, when you are.

But I think it is the Wizard who isn't quite ready to see me, to answer my question, or grant my wish.

Or his own.

But he will be.

And when he is, we'll both hear the terrible words that will rise from the emptiness of our conjoined heart, because we will both speak them, knowing the Road has at last come to an end, and a new beginning:

The Wizard will see you now.

Afterword

Well, we're certainly not in Kansas, anymore, are we.

You might be asking yourselves (if you've read this far – thanks if you have, and if you haven't, what are you doing here?) what's up with the Oz thing?

Dedicated Baum followers might already be petitioning the Nome King to take care of my sacrilegious butt. Judy Garland fans have probably contracted a Winkie hit squad.

Well, the quick answer is, I don't know.

I grew up with the MGM musical. Once a year the movie would come on television, and since there weren't many opportunities to watch fantasy movies in that era, I'd lay on the floor in front of the big old black and white television and watch it. Boy, was I surprised later to discover that most of it was shot in color!

My favorite part was always the flying monkeys. The witch's castle came in second.

The movie was part of my childhood playlist – Forbidden Planet, Creature From the Black Lagoon, The Thief of Bagdad, It Came From Outer Space, The 7th Voyage of Sinbad, War of the Worlds, Cat People, Godzilla, The Crawling Eye, House on Haunted

Hill, Invaders From Mars, Creation of the Humanoids, and everything else from the age of Creature Features. I admit, WoZ was an odd fit. But there was enough darkness to make me think what was happening had a hint of truth, and enough spectacle to keep my attention.

Maybe I identified with the witch (judging from Wicked's success as a book and Broadway musical, I'm not the only one), or the stranger-in-a-strange-land aspects of Dorothy's predicament.

Perhaps Dorothy's first act in the Land of Oz – witch murder – struck a familiar chord in the seething pre-adolescent fantasies of an only-child of immigrant parents misplaced in an American Oz.

Looking back, I think those other movies somehow tinted my perception of the MGM spectacle. I might not have been seeing the same movie everyone else was.

And then there was that episode of violent illness – a bad stomach virus that wiped me out for days – that erupted one night right around the time the flying monkeys swooped out of the sky. My fever dreams carried me to a hellish Oz – I'm not sure if I was the Tin Man, Cowardly Lion or King of the Flying Monkeys, but I definitely felt cursed by a cackling witch.

It was a few years before I went back to watching WoZ after that. And when I did finally return, the magic just wasn't there, anymore. Other miracles of imagination had come to television, and Man From U.N.C.L.E, Wild, Wild West, Twilight Zone and Outer Limits were delivering the kinds of goods I apparently needed. The British Invasion had also started, and I was paying attention to Gerry Anderson's puppet fantasies, Secret Agent and the Avengers.

The books never made a huge impact on me, I'm ashamed to say. I suppose I was already far too corrupted by the "glossy" darkness of video, and if I made it to the Nome King in the third book, his appearance probably just didn't impress me. My reading material tended toward bloody, gory myth, Burroughs' Mars series, Andre Norton and Robert Heinlein.

So the Wizard of Oz, mostly MGM with a dash of original Baum, has been simmering on the back burner of my brain for quite some time, absorbing textures and flavors from all the different spices and bits of raw meat tossed in over the years.

In the early 90's, the myth of the Hanged Man in the forest at the end of the Tin Woodsman scene started making the rounds. I also picked up an idea that the Winkie guards were chanting "no we love no one" as they marched into the witch's castle. I don't remember where I heard this reported, but years later Harlan Ellison made the same reference, so at the time I felt vindicated in my odd belief, privy to a secret, even sacred, piece of knowledge.

The phrase stuck with me. I gnawed at it, and it at me. So did the creepy idea of another level of "hanging man" evil lurking in the movie beyond witches and showmen shamans.

In May, 2002, an image came into my head with no connection to Oz – shells drifting to earth on parachutes like spider-babies. I guess that's what you get from watching too many nature shows. When I started typing, a boy took up the voice of the narrator. Not a particularly nice young fellow – perhaps a self born from that terrible stomach virus.

The title wanted that image and the boy. I didn't stand in the way, and eventually "no we love no one" nested in an obsession with the movie by the story's "others" which also provided a kind of reason for what happened in the story.

I received good feedback from the piece when it was published, which inspired me to think a bit more about this whole Oz thing. I felt there were other ways to play with the mythic material, more to say about people through the warped lens of my own, personal WoZ.

I leaned a bit on the original Baum with the second story, as well as the Witch and the King of the Flying Monkeys. I wanted to play with the "wicked" parts of the story, in this world and in the Land of Oz. And, yes, okay, Sam Peckinpah was an inspiration. The title possessed me, what can I say.

The third title also possessed me, just a little line from the movie that, for me, captured both the wonder and the terror of an audience with the Wizard. For me, the first story was a tale of the apocalypse and the second more of a psychological fantasy, so I followed the yellow brick road leading to greater interior landscapes and found trauma and a quest for its resolution.

Well, that's what I make of them, for whatever that's worth.

Hopefully, whatever you made of these stories, you had fun.

I certainly did writing them.

February, 2008

www.ingramcontent.com/pod-product-compliance
Lightning Source LLC
Chambersburg PA
CBHW030207130726

47898CB00012B/912